THE SUICIDE SQUAD:
THE SUICIDE SQUAD'S DAWN PATROL
AND OTHER STORIES

ACE G-MAN

THE SUICIDE SQUAD'S DAWN PATROL

AND OTHER STORIES

By Emile C. Tepperman

POPULAR PUBLICATIONS • 2022

THE MASKED MARKSMAN'S
COMMAND PERFORMANCE

"PARDON ME!" said the tall man. "So clumsy of me. This train is lurching so—"

"It's all right," Ed Race said, as the train swung around a curve once more, throwing them all together again in the narrow corridor. "I don't mind being bumped into. I don't even mind having my foot stepped on. But I *do* mind my pocket picked!"

He seized hold of the tall man's wrist, and twisted it hard.

The train was speeding through the night along the flat coastal plain of the Carolinas, bound from Miami to New York. Ed, returning from an engagement at the Seabright Theatre in Miami, was due to open at the Clyde, in New York, tomorrow evening. His Masked Marksman number had been advertised there for weeks in advance.

Ed had gone to the club car for a midnight snack. He never could sleep on a train anyway, and he had whiled away an hour in there, talking with the steward, and with another passenger also a night owl apparently. Now, on his way back to his own car, these two had been waiting in the corridor of the Pullman compartment—the tall dark one, handsome and lithe; and the smaller one, who looked more like a youngster running away from college to enlist, than like the accomplice of a pickpocket.

Ed Race liked the looks of both these fellows. Their eyes were keen, shrewd—and apparently honest. But there was no doubt

that the tall one had deliberately feigned bumping into him, and had lifted Ed's wallet from his inside breast pocket. The man had done it quite skillfully. No ordinary person would have detected the theft. But Ed Race, in addition to being a star headliner on the Partages Vaudeville Circuit, had made a hobby of studying criminology. The two heavy hair-trigger .45 revolvers which he carried in his twin shoulder holsters had often sung their deep-throated symphonies in battles with criminals, as well as in the phenomenal Masked Marksman routine which he performed on the stage, from coast to coast.

He was a little bit surprised now, and disgusted with himself, because he hadn't tagged these two as criminals. At first glance, they had appeared likable enough chaps.

Nevertheless, he twisted the tall man's wrist hard enough to make him drop the wallet.

Ed swooped down and picked it up, keeping his eyes on both of them.

The tall man did not appear frightened or worried at the thought of having been caught in the act of committing a misdemeanor. He said gloomily to his companion, "I muffed it, Steve! What do you know about that? I must be losing my touch!"

The gray eyes of the little fellow flickered. He didn't seem angry at his pal's bungling. "It was the train, Dan," he said, consolingly. "You can't expect to do a job like that, when the train dances all around the track."

Ed looked at them in puzzled fashion. He had never heard crooks talk like that.

"See here, you fellows," he said. "I ought to turn you in for this. But I'm going to forget it. Scram. You both should be ashamed of yourselves. A couple of nice chaps like you ought to be able to make an honest living—instead of being common thieves!"

The tall dark one, who had been addressed as Dan by his companion, flushed angrily. Then he immediately smiled. "It's darned white of you to let us go, mister." He jerked his head at

The plane was down to three hundred now, and the bomb would be released in an instant!

his companion, and they both crowded close against Ed. *"But we want to see what's inside that wallet!"*

Steve, the smaller one, took a small automatic pistol from the right-hand pocket of his coat. He held it at his side, and smiled significantly at Ed.

"Do we make ourselves plain?" he asked softly.

Ed Race understood now, that these two men were far more dangerous than they seemed. If they were criminals, then they belonged in the highest brackets of underworld society.

Why they should want his wallet so badly, he couldn't understand. True, he carried several hundred dollars in it. But to men like these, that kind of money should be only chicken feed. What he did understand very clearly though, was that he wasn't going to let himself be held up by them, or anybody else.

THE CORRIDOR in which they were standing was narrow. Since this was an all-compartment car, the corridor was on the left side, with the doors of the compartments on the right. The people in those rooms were no doubt asleep.

Ed looked at the gun in Steve's hand. Then he deliberately put the wallet in his side coat pocket.

Steve sighed. He snicked the safety catch off his automatic. The tall one reached for Ed's arm.

"Sorry, pal—"

Ed Race smiled grimly. He took a swift step backward and threw himself into a back flip. He had done that back flip a thousand times, on the stages of theatres in every city in the country. It was part of the routine of his Masked Marksman number. In that act, he juggled six .45 hair-trigger revolvers, like the ones now resting in his shoulder holsters. When he had all six of them high in the air, he would go into a back flip, come out of it and catch the revolvers two at the time, as they came down. And as he caught them, he would fire each at a row of candles thirty feet across the stage. In ten years, he had never missed one of those candles.

True, the corridor here was much narrower than the stage of a theatre, and the train was swaying from side to side. Also, it would hardly be possible for the little one to miss, with that automatic of his. Ed had performed this same trick many a time in the past—off the stage—when his life hung in the balance. But even as he went into the flip, he realized that these two men were not of a calibre to be confused by the trick. Nevertheless, he meant to go through with it.

The few moments that he was in the air seemed like hours, for he expected at any moment to hear the spiteful bark of that automatic, and to feel the jar of a slug.

But no shot came. If they were waiting for him to land before shooting, then they had an unpleasant surprise in store for themselves!

Ed's face was grim as he came to his feet in the narrow corridor, fifteen feet away from the two men. He was facing them now, with his two revolvers in his hands. That draw of his, which he performed daily on the stage, had not lost one iota of its blinding swiftness.

He thrust the heavy muzzles out at the two men, who had been running toward him, the smaller one in the lead. They both stopped short.

Ed's two revolvers covered them, and the automatic of the one called Steve covered him, in turn.

The three of them stood that way, like a tableau of stone.

Ed could have fired both his revolvers as he came to his feet, and cut those two men down. But he knew also, that Steve could have shot, just as easily. Therefore, he held his fire.

"Well," he said, "what do we do now?"

He saw the faces of the two men relax into smiles. They were both looking at him with genuine admiration.

"That was a neat stunt you just pulled!" said the tall, dark one. "I never saw anything as neat as that—except once, in a vaude-ville theatre."

"Thanks," Ed said drily.

"It'll be a shame to kill you," said the little one. "It's too bad you're a spy. I didn't think a Nazi would have the guts to do what you just did."

"Nazi!" exclaimed Ed. "You're calling me a Nazi spy?"

"That's right," said Steve. "You're von Bernhoff."

"And you're crazy!" Ed told him. Then his eyes flickered. "Ah! I get it! You're trying to squirm out of this, by claiming you thought I was a spy! You're just a couple of pickpockets, trying to squeeze out of a tough spot!"

The tall dark one made a wry face. "And you're just a Nazi spy, trying to hand out a stiff bluff."

Ed grinned. He wiggled the two revolvers. "When you have two things like these in your hands, my friend, it's no bluff!"

Steve grinned right back at him, and wiggled the automatic. "This is no bluff either, pal."

ED WAS puzzled. The more he saw of these fellows, the more he felt it was ridiculous to tag them as cheap crooks. But the fact remained that they had tried to pick his pocket. Ordinarily, a pickpocket, when caught, will whine. These men, however, were very far from whining.

"Well, we can't stand here all night," Ed said. "The train will be pulling into Richmond pretty soon."

"We mean to see the inside of that wallet!" Steve told him tightly.

"Sorry," said Ed. "You can't get it."

He saw a peculiar gleam in the eyes of the two men.

"Oh, yes we can!" said the tall dark one. Then he added gently, speaking to some one behind Ed, "Take him gently, Johnny. He's not a bad fellow!"

Ed said disgustedly, "Now listen, if you think you can pull a moth-eaten one like that—" He stopped abruptly, as he felt the chill touch of cold steel against the back of his neck.

"This," said a deep bass voice behind him, "is a thing that shoots. It's thirty-eight calibre—more than a third of an inch. Imagine the kind of hole it'll make in the back of your head if I shoot!"

Ed Race stood very still. He did not lower his revolvers. He saw the grim smiles of amusement on the faces of Steve and Dan.

"So there are three of you!" he said. "Three husky men, all thieves. Well, you've picked the wrong victim this time. Observe, gentlemen, that the two revolvers I'm holding have hair triggers. Observe how my fingers are curled around these triggers.

If I should be shot from behind—or if I should even be jarred, say by a blow on the head—my fingers would would contract by reflex action. These two revolvers would go off. Notice that they are pointing at your stomachs, gentlemen. Notice also, that they are forty-five calibre—almost a half inch in diameter. Can you imagine what nasty holes would be in your stomachs if your friend behind me should do anything rash?"

Steve and Dan studied him for a moment, with a new sort of respect.

"I believe he means it!" Steve murmured.

"I'll be damned!" said Dan.

"It's a deadlock!" said the deep voice behind Ed.

"I have an idea!" exclaimed the tall, dark one, suddenly. He looked at Ed. "See here, von Bernhoff—"

"Don't call me von Bernhoff," Ed said coldly.

"I'll call you whatever I like," Dan told him. "Whatever your name is, I have a proposition to make to you. There are three of us, and only one of you. If we start shooting, you'll surely die. And at least one of us will be alive—to get your wallet. Now that doesn't sound fair to me. We despise all you slimy Nazi spies. But when we meet a man with guts, we like to give him a fighting chance—a sporting chance."

"It sounds like a bunch of bellywash," Ed said. "But go ahead. What's your proposition?"

"We'll make this an even fight," Dan offered. "Two of us will get out of this car. We'll lock the doors at both ends from the inside. My friends will go, and I'll be left here alone with you. Each of us with two guns in his hand. We'll shoot it out, one to one. If you win, you can get off this train, and no one will stop you. If I win—" he shrugged—"that's the chance you have to take."

"I don't get it," Ed said. "I think you're sincere about that proposition. I can see it in your eyes. But I don't understand why you're willing to shoot it out for the contents of my wallet. I only have three or four hundred dollars in it—"

"Don't act stupid!" the tall, dark one said impatiently. "We know you're the cleverest man in the German Secret Service. And you know damned well why we want that wallet!"

Ed's eyes narrowed. With the cold muzzle of the gun at the back of his neck, and with his own two revolvers centered on Dan and Steve, he spoke slowly and thoughtfully.

"Are you chaps trying to tell me that you're in the U.S. Secret Service?"

"F.B.I.," said Steve.

"Just to keep the record straight," Dan added, and raised his hand to his inner coat pocket. Ed made no objection. He watched him like a hawk as he withdrew an identification card case and flipped it open. Ed looked at the card which was exposed, under a cellophane cover. It had a picture of Dan, stamped with the seal of the Department of Justice. The card read:

"The bearer, Daniel Murdoch, is a Special Agent of the Federal Bureau of Investigation, of the United States Department of Justice."

"Well, I'll be damned!" said Ed.

Slowly, he lowered his two revolvers. Then he crossed his arms and slid them into their holsters.

Immediately, the cold muzzle was removed from the back of his neck.

"Looks like a truce!" said the deep bass voice behind him.

Ed turned around to get a look at the fellow who had been covering him. He saw a big man, powerfully built, with the shoulders of a stevedore, and hair that was as red as a ripe carrot.

The big man bowed. "Johnny Kerrigan, at your service, *Herr* von Bernhoff," he said.

"Go to hell!" Ed said hotly. "I'm not von Bernhoff—"

He stopped abruptly, as a sudden light of understanding gleamed in his eyes. "Johnny Kerrigan!" He turned around to face the tall, dark one. "Dan Murdoch!" Then he glanced at the little one, who looked like a kid that had run away from college to enlist. "Then you must be Stephen Klaw!"

Steve grinned. "You've got the names right!"

"The Suicide Squad!" Ed exclaimed. "Kerrigan, Murdoch and Klaw! I've heard about you fellows. No wonder I couldn't bring myself to believe that you were cheap sneak thieves!"

"Thanks for the compliment," Dan Murdoch said drily. "And we find it hard to believe that a guy with guts like yours is a Nazi spy."

"But dammit I tell you I'm not!" Ed told him hotly. "Where did you get the idea that I'm a Nazi spy?"

"We were tipped off," Johnny Kerrigan boomed.

"By whom?"

"By a dame. Greta Frisch. Ever hear of her?"

"Sorry," said Ed. "I never heard the name." He saw that all three of them were watching him keenly. "Am I supposed to know this Greta Frisch?"

DAN MURDOCH grinned. "You sure are! She worked for your spy organization. She's just turned against the Nazis. We arrested her in Miami yesterday, and she broke down and gave us the whole story. This train is supposed to be carrying two special freight cars with the first batch of the new high explosive we're making for the Air Force. The two cars that were hooked on at Jacksonville. Well, Greta told us that *you* were going to board the train, and give a signal, somewhere between Jacksonville and Richmond, and that a hidden plane which would be stalking the train, would dive bomb it—*after* you jumped off."

Ed looked at them queerly. "And you thought *I* was von Bern-hoff?"

"We still think so!" Steve Klaw grinned. "Greta told us you were going to ignite a powder, that you're carrying in your wallet. It will make a flare, which will guide the plane to this train. She described you to us. Five-foot-ten, gray eyes, tan overcoat, brown slouch hat. She even told us you were wearing that tan-and-gray striped necktie!"

"Not only that," Dan Murdoch interrupted, "but when I picked your pocket I felt those holstered revolvers. That cinched it."

"You see," Johnny Kerrigan explained, "we figured we'd take that powder out of your wallet, and substitute some bicarbonate of soda for it. Then, when you tried to make the flare, nothing would happen, and we'd grab you in the act. We figure you've

11

got some accomplice on board the train, and that you'll all try to leave before the plane attacks."

"Now let me get this right," said Ed. "Is my real name supposed to be von Bernhoff?"

"Right," said Stephen Klaw. "And you're traveling under a false name—Alex Wheeler."

Ed shook his head. He had heard much about Kerrigan, Murdoch and Klaw. They were called the Suicide Squad, among those who knew the inside of things that happened in the F.B.I. Three more daring and clever agents did not exist in the service of any country in the world.

"Boys," he said quietly, "you're knocking at the wrong door. I'm not von Bernhoff. This Greta Frisch has given you a song and dance. She described me, because she wanted you to concentrate on some one else, while the real von Bernhoff does his stuff. Here. I'll prove it to you." He took his wallet out of his pocket, and handed it to Dan Murdoch. "See for yourself!"

Murdoch took the wallet. He opened it, and thumbed through the cards. He let a low whistle escape him. He held up a couple of the cards. One of them was an automobile operator's license, issued in the name of *Alex Wheeler!* Another was a membership card in the defunct German-American Bund, also in the name of Alex Wheeler. And then, he carefully drew out a small glassine envelope, containing a white powder!

Murdoch scowled at Ed Race. "So, my dear von Bernhoff," he said, "this is the end!"

ED'S FOREHEAD was creased in perplexity. Suddenly he snapped his fingers. "I get it now! I gave my suit to the train valet to press, this evening. I forgot to take the wallet out. Some one must have changed the papers in it!"

"Hah!" said Johnny Kerrigan. "You'll have to do better than that. Come on in here!"

He opened the door of one of the compartments, and Ed saw a beautiful blond woman seated inside. She looked up as the door opened, and a smile appeared upon her full, sensuous lips.

"Otto!" she exclaimed, looking straight at Ed.

Johnny Kerrigan said to her, "Greta Frisch, do you know this man?"

"Why of course," she replied. "This is Otto von Bernhoff."

"You switched papers on me!" Ed exclaimed. "Tell them where the real von Bernhoff is!"

Her blue eyes opened wide. "You are the real von Bernhoff— and I am betraying you. I am sick of working for Germany. I will become an American citizen!"

Ed turned desperately to Dan Murdoch. "She's lying, Murdoch. If what you've told me is true, the real von Bernhoff is at liberty on the train at this moment, and he'll signal that plane. This train will be destroyed. You've got to believe me!"

"Indeed!" Dan Murdoch said. "And in that case, who would *you* be?"

"You've heard of the Masked Marksman?" Ed asked swiftly.

"Of course. He's the guy that does the phenomenal gun-jug-gling and marksmanship act—"

"That's right. Well, *I'm* the Masked Marksman."

"I've seen the act," Johnny Kerrigan said. "It's a wow. But you're not the guy. You're von Bernhoff—"

"You saw the back flip I just did," Ed interrupted, addressing himself to Murdoch and Klaw. "Remember seeing it on the stage?"

"Yes," Klaw said thoughtfully. "But that doesn't prove you're the Masked Marksman. He wore a mask—"

"That's right," Ed said. "I always wear a mask. My name is Race. Ed Race."

Greta Frisch began to laugh. "It will do you no good, Otto. Your geese is cooked—"

Ed swung away from her, to face Kerrigan and Murdoch and Klaw. "Look here—I don't mind being called von Bernhoff, or anything else. I don't care what happens to me. But I don't want to see this train dive-bombed." He took a deep breath. "Suppose I *prove* to you that I'm Ed Race?"

"How?" Steve Klaw demanded concisely.

Ed brushed past Greta Frisch, and raised the window blind. He pointed ahead, to the lights of a local station which they were approaching. It was manifest that the train was not going to stop at this station, for it was tearing ahead at full speed.

"See that station ahead?" he demanded. "We'll be passing it in two minutes. See that string of lights over at the far end, past the local tracks?"

"Yes," said Dan Murdoch, somewhat guardedly.

"They're fifty feet away from this track, aren't they?"

"Yes."

"Could any of you three hit all of those lights as the train flashes past—with a forty-five?"

"No!" Stephen Klaw answered promptly and frankly. "That's

14

impossible. Maybe with a Garand rifle—but not with a revolver. Not even the best marksman in the world would do that—"

"The Masked Marksman can do it!" Ed said.

They were already streaking into the station, and the first of that string of lights was coming abreast of the locomotive up ahead.

"Will you trust me with guns in my hand?" Ed asked swiftly.

"Go ahead!" Dan Murdoch said suddenly, from behind him. "I'll keep you covered. But go ahead. I have a hunch—"

"Thanks!" Ed whispered.

Hardly had the word left his lips, than his two hands crossed and uncrossed over his chest, and the two heavy .45's were out. The motion was so fast that Dan Murdoch and his two companions blinked.

With another swift, powerful motion, Ed smashed out the window glass with the barrel of one of the weapons. Their car was just coming abreast of the row of lights.

HE DIDN'T seem to aim. He must throw down both guns and fire them simultaneously. His actions appeared easy and nonchalant. In reality, however, he was so tautly strung that every nerve and fibre of his body was atingle. He knew he couldn't afford to miss. He must convince these three hard-bitten fighting men that he was the Masked Marksman; not von Bernhoff.

Both guns began to thunder in unison. They bucked and roared in Ed's hands, as the train raced past that row of lights. And with each swift double explosion, two of those bulbs were shattered into blackness. Down the line the shots clicked, with the military precision of a parade review. And as the train flashed past the station, every last one of those lights was extinguished!

Ed Race drew a deep breath into his lungs, and lowered his empty, smoking revolvers. He looked at Kerrigan, Murdoch and Klaw.

"Well?" he said.

"My aunt's Sunday hat!" whispered Stephen Klaw. "I've never seen shooting like that!"

"By God," said Dan Murdoch, "a guy who can shoot like that—*can't* be a Nazi!"

Johnny Kerrigan grunted. "The people in that town must be thinking they've had a blitzkrieg!"

As the train sped along, never reducing its pace, the wind whipped into the compartment through the open window, mingled with cinders and soot. Suddenly, from somewhere in the rear, there was a flashing explosion, and a flare brightened the sky for hundreds of yards in every direction. It was far down at the rear of the train, somewhere near the observation car. But the train did not leave that flare behind. It travelled right along with it.

"There's the signal!" Steve Klaw exclaimed. "He's ignited that powder, on the rear platform of the observation car!"

"That means the plane will be diving in a couple of minutes!" Steve Klaw said tightly.

From her seat, Greta Frisch sprang up, with a sudden deathly pallor upon her face.

"Let me out!" she screamed. "I do not want to die—"

Dan Murdoch gripped her wrist. "Not so fast, sister," he said grimly. "You were playing your own game with us right along, weren't you? This man isn't von Bernhoff, is he? You put us on to him, only so that the real von Bernhoff would be free to do his work tonight. That's true—isn't it?"

"No, no," she screamed. "Let me get off—"

"Let's all stay and be bombed!" said Johnny Kerrigan.

"Suits me," said Ed Race, his eyes fixed on the woman.

She stared from one to the other of them, with dawning fear and terror. "You—you are not going to get off? We will all be killed!"

"That's right, sister," said Dan Murdoch.

Her face assumed a greenish tint as she saw that they meant it.

"No, no! I will tell you everything. It is true. I changed the wallets. The real von Bernhoff is in the club car. A thin man—"

Ed Race snapped his fingers. "That's the chap I was talking to in the club car!"

High above the rumble of the train, they heard the drone of an airplane engine.

"There's the bomber!" said Dan Murdoch. "He won't dive for a couple of minutes, yet. He'll want to give von Bernhoff time to get off. Let's go!"

Stephen Klaw and Johnny Kerrigan swung out into the corridor with him. Forgotten was Greta Frisch.

"Hey!" yelled Ed Race. "I'm coming, too—"

All four of them raced down to the rear end door of the Pullman. Ed swiftly reloaded his guns as he ran.

"We're going up on the roof," Murdoch said. "We'll see if we can't give that bomber what-for!"

Suddenly, there was a screaming whistle, as some one pulled the emergency bell cord, in one of the rear cars. The engineer up front responded instantly, and the train ground to screeching stop.

"It's von Bernhoff!" Klaw said. "He's stopped the train so the bomber can have an easy target—and so he can get off!"

THEY SCRAMBLED out on to the vestibule, and Johnny Kerrigan yanked the lever which opened the door. Then, as one man, they swung on Ed Race. Almost in chorus they said, "Race, we apologize. You're a right guy. So long."

Then Johnny Kerrigan cupped his hands, and Dan Murdoch climbed up, reaching the roof, and scrambling up on top.

"Nix," said Ed. "I'm going up there with you. You need a good marksman—"

"Sorry," said Klaw. "Your job is to get out there and grab von Bernhoff. He'll probably have a couple more accomplices. That job will be dangerous enough. Now scram. This is war, and these are orders!"

"Very good, sir!" Ed said, saluting.

He leaped down to the darkness of the roadbed.

"See you in hell, Race!" Kerrigan and Murdoch and Klaw called after him.

Ed grinned. "That's a date, you lugs!" he called back.

He saw that they had all reached the roof of the car, and were standing upright, with their guns in their hands. High above, the plane, a weird specter in the night sky, was wheeling into a power dive. It began to come down, its motor roaring.

Ed turned away from that sight. Whatever happened, he knew his job was elsewhere. The darkness was being eerily illuminated by the flare powder at the rear. By its light, he saw three dark shapes running away from the train, then start to climb the embankment.

Ed grinned tightly.

"Stop!" he shouted.

But his voice was hardly audible above the screaming of that diving plane, and the thundering guns of the Suicide Squad, on the roof of the car.

Coolly, Ed lined up his two revolvers. Those three fleeing figures were an easy target for him. He fired once with his right-hand revolver, and twice with the left-hand one.

The two men and one woman fell prone on the slope of the embankment, like ten-pins, their legs shot out from under them. Deliberately, Ed had aimed at their knees. He wanted them alive.

Then he swung around and raised his head. Only seconds had elapsed, but the plane was already down to five hundred feet. In the light of the flare, he could see the bomb rack underneath it, and he could clearly see the pilot's head in the cockpit. The pilot was leaning forward, apparently with his hand on the bomb release.

On the roof of the car, Kerrigan and Murdoch and Klaw were firing, carefully, coolly, and the windshield was cracked but not splintered. They were directly in front of the nose of the plane, and therefore couldn't get a shot at the pilot from the side, which offered a little more possibility.

Ed Race raised his revolvers, and joined in the fight. Passengers were streaming out of the train, in huddled confusion, running away from the strafing attack. But those four—Kerrigan and Murdoch and Klaw on the roof of the car, and Ed Race on the ground—did not give an inch.

The plane was down to three hundred now, and the bomb would be released in an instant. Its nose was pointing directly downward, and Ed sighted his revolvers for that impossible target. He fired four times, and he didn't know which of the four shots hit. But suddenly there was an earth-shattering explosion, and all the heavens seemed to close upon themselves in a blinding tornado of crashing light and sound. The train rocked on its tracks, and Ed Race was thrown off his feet. Bits of metal and shreds of airplane wings and motor catapulted in all directions.

Those bullets in the nose had detonated the bomb. Its driving, explosive force had been expended far enough from its intended target so that the fragments which reached the ground were only those which fell, after the explosion. They did little damage.

Ed Race got to his feet, feeling slightly drunk. He looked around. There was no longer any plane in the air. The pilot and his vehicle of death had been obliterated by their own cargo.

Ed saw Kerrigan, Murdoch and Klaw picking themselves up from the ground, where they had been hurled. They saw him, and grinned.

Ed grinned back at them. "If this is hell," he said, "it's not so bad. Glad to see you lugs again."

Stephen Klaw spoke for the three of them. "Same here!" he said. "It's not so bad at that!"

THE SUICIDE SQUAD'S
DAWN PATROL

CHAPTER 1
THE MESSAGE

THE PRETTY Filipino girl in the starched white uniform stopped Stephen Klaw at the corner. She had a charming smile and a dimple in her left cheek.

"Contribution to the Red Cross, sir?" she asked.

"Sure," said Steve. He dug in his pocket for change, flipped her a quarter.

"Do you know what time it is?" he asked her.

The girl stiffened. "No," she said. "Do you?"

"It's time to strike!" said Stephen Klaw.

The girl's eyes flashed. "That's the code word the F.B.I. gave me. You must be Stephen Klaw!"

"That's right," he said. He dropped a coin into the contribution box, and she stepped close to him and pinned a Red Cross button on his lapel.

"It's the third house from the corner," she said swiftly. "Number Thirteen. He's waiting for you—in the top floor rear apartment. But it's no use. You'll never get to him. They've found out that you're coming. They've set a trap for you. I don't know exactly what, but they mean to kill you and Kerrigan and Murdoch!"

23

Kerrigan and Murdoch began to shoot, coolly, deliberately, at the leaders of that throng.

Stephen Klaw smiled. He nodded to her, as if thanking her for the button, and moved on. He did not even glance at Number Thirteen as he passed it. Nor did he seem to be interested in the motley conglomeration of faces which he passed on the street—Puerto Ricans, Filipinos, Haitians, Dominicans, half-castes and quarter-castes, with the blood of a dozen different races boiling hotly in their veins.

This was the so-called Spanish quarter of the city, a veritable rabbit-warren of intrigue, where treachery and sabotage made their beds side by side with murder and hate. A quarter of a million people lived here in this sprawling section half a mile square. Most of them were peaceable men and women, who wanted nothing better than to be allowed to live and work in the United States. But there were others—the agents of every Axis power—who moved boldly in this melting pot, secure in their anonymity; secure in their knowledge that to seek them here would be like looking for the proverbial needle in the haystack.

Klaw walked a little farther down the block and paused beside a parked car, ostensibly to light a cigarette.

Johnny Kerrigan was seated at the wheel of the car, his head sunk on his powerful shoulders in an attitude of meditation. Actually he was peering into a small mirror which he held in the palm of his left hand. By using that mirror, he had been able to follow Stephen Klaw's progress up the street. He did not show by any sign that he was aware of Steve's existence.

Klaw lit his cigarette, took a deep puff. "The fat's in the fire, Johnny," he said. "They know we're coming to find Balbo. They've set a trap."

Johnny Kerrigan put the hand mirror away and turned around, grinning. "I never did like this *hush-hush stuff*, anyway!"

"Balbo is in Number Thirteen, top floor rear," Steve told him. "Suppose I take the front, you take the back, and let Dan come in through the roof. He can go in the house on the far corner, and work his way across the roofs."

"Sold," said Johnny. "Dan is down the street. I'll contact him. Give us ten minutes to get set, and then you go in. The three of us will try to meet inside Number Thirteen."

"Okay, mope," said Steve. "But remember, no Boy Scout stuff. Remember what the Chief said: One of us must get to Manuel Balbo tonight—*at any cost!*"

"Right!" said Johnny Kerrigan, starting the car. "See you in hell, Shrimp!"

"Not if I see you first!" Steve called after him.

HE WATCHED the car pull down the block; saw the tall, spare figure of Dan Murdoch detach itself from the shadows and get in. He waited until the car disappeared around the corner. Then he dug both hands deep in his coat pockets, and started back toward Number Thirteen.

He saw that the Filipino girl was no longer at the corner. There were no police in evidence, for the two big fires along the docks had denuded the rest of the city of its uniformed force. Across the street, a fight was going on, between a wiry mulatto and a big Jamaican. A crowd had gathered round the two fighters across the street, but no one offered to interfere.

Elsewhere along the street, men and women were walking, talking and laughing. But underneath that surface gaiety, there was a sense of acute tension. These people were aware of the undercurrents of intrigue and treachery which crept through the district. They were afraid....

Steve's watch showed that five minutes of the allotted ten had passed. He was only four or five doors away from Number Thirteen, and he must not reach the front door for five minutes more. The success of their plan depended upon accurate timing. He stopped at the curb to watch the fight across the street.

As he turned, something *whirred* past his ear. A little Filipino boy, who had just started to run across to the opposite side, threw up his arms and screamed, then fell headlong in the gutter.

The boy had been only a few feet from Steve. Whatever it was that had *whirred* past Steve's ear, had struck that lad.

Stephen Klaw leaped toward the boy, and at the same moment, something else whizzed past him and buried itself in the boy's body. Steve swung around, drawing from his right-hand pocket the automatic he had been holding there. His eyes, narrowed and keen, swept back along the route which that missile must have taken; his glance rested on the first floor window of Number Nineteen, which was only three houses from the one toward which he had been going. The window was in darkness, but he spotted the shadowy figure which was visible, crouching against the sill, with a long tube at its mouth.

Steve fired almost at the same time that he saw the figure. His single shot blasted above the clamor which had risen in the street, and he saw the figure in the window topple backward. The tube fell out the window, dropped to the sidewalk almost at Steve's feet.

Steve stooped and snatched it up. He stuck it into his pocket, and swung toward the wounded boy. His eyes became bleak. That frail, skinny body was still and rigid.

Klaw had no doubt that those two poisoned darts which had done their work so swiftly had been meant for himself. The unfortunate lad had died from them, in a matter of seconds.

There was a milling crowd in the street now, and fierce eyes, smoldering with hate, were turned upon Stephen Klaw. A narrow-chested man with a mottled face pointed a finger at

Klaw, and then at the dead boy. He shouted something in a strange, unintelligible language, but it was plain to see what he meant. He was telling the crowd that Klaw had killed the boy!

The crowd surged forward, but did not come too close, because of the automatic which Steve still held in his hand.

Just then, a big Haitian woman came running down the street. She pushed through the crowd, and dropped to her knees beside the pitiful, dead body. A long, unearthly wail escaped her as she threw herself across the limp figure.

The narrow-chested man shouted something else, and the crowd uttered a roar of rage. This time it surged forward purposefully. The narrow-chested man brandished a revolver, but did not take the lead.

Klaw's face was grim. His time was up. He had to get into Number Thirteen, and not even this must be allowed to stop him. He raised his automatic, and shot the narrow-chested man in the shoulder, and the fellow went hurtling back into the crowd, screaming.

That stopped the bloodthirsty crowd for a moment, and Steve took advantage of its hesitation. He turned and sprinted for Number Thirteen.

The mob, thinking that he was trying to make his escape out of the block, uttered a deep roar of rage, and started after him. Klaw smiled twistedly. He swung into the entrance of Number Thirteen, and slammed the door shut almost in the faces of the first of the pursuers.

There was a glass panel in the door. Steve grinned at them

through the glass; he raised his automatic. Those in the forefront of the mob squealed with fright and backed away.

THE HALL was lighted by a single bulb, but its illumination was sufficient for Steve to see the powerful figure of Johnny Kerrigan, approaching from the rear.

"Hi, Shrimp," said Johnny. "What gives?"

Steve jerked his thumb at the mob outside.

"I brought some company," he said.

"They sound like nice people," Kerrigan grinned. "Dan must be at the roof by this time. Let's go."

He started up the stairs, drawing his revolver.

Stephen Klaw fell in step beside him. They mounted the first flight without opposition. The bloodcurdling shouts of the mob in the street were growing ever louder, though. As they reached the second landing, a door at the front was kicked open, and a machine-gun began to stutter. The staccato chattering of that rapid-fire gun filled the whole house with its vicious patter. The stinging slugs swept high over the heads of Klaw and Kerrigan, then swung downward as the gunner in the front room adjusted his aim.

But the swift ambuscade did not catch Kerrigan and Klaw flatfooted. Their reaction was almost as swift as the first patter of sound from the machine-gun. The guns in their hands began to blast, hurling twin streams of lead to the doorway.

They didn't have to adjust their aim. Their guns fired neither too high nor too low.

Too often had their lives depended upon the accuracy of the first shot in a battle. They had learned to make that first shot count. And they had worked together so long that they didn't have to guess what the other would do, or hope that the other would do the right thing. Steve, who was on the left, took the left-hand half of the doorway, spacing his shots up and down its length; while Johnny did the same thing with the other half.

The deafening din of blasting guns shook the frail old house as if it were being rocked by a quake. And then, suddenly, the machine-gun faltered in its staccato music. There was a second of silence, and a single burst blasted high, the slugs smashing into the ceiling of the hall. Then there was a crash as the machine-gun clattered to the floor. The bulb which lit the corridor had been blasted out of existence, but even in the darkness, Steve and Johnny saw the shadowy bulk of the gunner's figure as he fell forward over his weapon.

Kerrigan and Klaw leaped forward, shoulder to shoulder down the hall. They reached the doorway at the same time. Within that room they saw two more figures, leaping forward to pick up the machine-gun. Kerrigan's thirty-eight and Klaw's lighter automatic spoke simultaneously, and there were no more enemies left in the room.

As the thunder and din of the echoing gunfire died away, Johnny Kerrigan brought out his flashlight and swung the beam down upon the bodies at their feet. All three dead men were small-boned, with small and dainty hands and black, oily hair. Their faces were long and narrow, yellow, with high narrow foreheads and small eyes.

"Japs!" said Johnny Kerrigan. "They were all supposed to have been rounded up!"

"There must be plenty more of them hiding out all over the city," Steve said. He swung around. "Let's go. Dan must be through the roof by this time. I wonder what he's running into—"

As if in answer to his question, a short series of gun blasts sounded from above.

Johnny and Steve went up the next flight of stairs like a pair of comets.

Like all other tenement houses in the district, this one was a crowded beehive of humanity, with six flats on each floor, and an unbelievable number of men, women and children jammed into each flat. But not a single one of them came out into the hallway. All the doors remained closed.

SOME ONE had put out the lights on the upper floors, and Johnny's flashlight, lancing up the stairs, showed nothing on the third floor landing. But the shots up above continued.

Kerrigan and Klaw reached the top floor landing unopposed, and the flashlight in Johnny's hand swept along the hall to reveal half a dozen little yellow men, crouching under the skylight, staring upward. Two of those little men had automatics. The other four had blowguns just like the one in Steve's pocket. They had the tubes at their lips, and were aiming up at the open skylight, as if waiting for a chance to send their deadly missiles winging on their way.

As Kerrigan and Klaw reached the landing, they saw a spurt of orange flame from above, accompanied by the roar of Dan Murdoch's revolver. One of the Japs screamed and toppled forward. At the same time, the other Japs swung to meet Kerrigan and Klaw. It was apparent that they had not expected an attack from below, for they had been sure that their little ambuscade on the first floor would effectively stop anyone coming in from the street.

The deadly blowguns lined up on Johnny and Steve, while the two Japs with revolvers opened a steady barrage toward the skylight, aimed at keeping Murdoch away from the opening.

Kerrigan and Klaw disdained to duck, or to scramble for safety. They stood shoulder to shoulder in the narrow corridor, guns in both hands, and pulled their triggers coolly and methodically. In their right-hand guns they had only two or three shots left, but there was a full load in each of their second guns. Kerrigan had dropped his flashlight, and it lay with its beam athwart the hall, casting a weird glow upon the ghastly battle.

The air was filled with thunder and the fumes of cordite. As if by unspoken agreement, Klaw took the dart-blowers, while Kerrigan aimed at the two Japs whose revolvers were blazing at the skylight.

Klaw's slugs smashed into those kneeling Japs with the tubes in their mouths, sending them crashing backward into their fellows; while Kerrigan's bullets found the gunmen with unerring accuracy.

Up above, Dan Murdoch was not to be kept from the skylight by the barrage. His long and supple figure came through the opening, both his guns blazing straight down as he jumped. He landed feet-first upon the last of the Japs, smashing the fellow to the floor. Then Dan came nimbly to his feet and faced Kerrigan and Klaw, who had ceased firing.

There was not a Jap left standing. The three G-men grinned at each other.

"Nice work, guys!" Dan Murdoch said.

Below, in the street, the angry roar of the mob surged up like an echo out of hell.

Dan Murdoch looked inquiringly at the other two.

Steve grinned thinly. "Just some nice people who want my scalp. Come on, let's get Balbo!"

He stepped across the dead Japs, and stopped in front of the door of the rear apartment. Johnny Kerrigan came and stood alongside him, playing his flashlight on the door. They both drew their breath in sharply.

The door was riddled by bullet holes.

"They played a machine-gun on it!" Dan Murdoch exclaimed.

Kerrigan kicked the door open, and strode into the room, followed by Klaw and Murdoch.

A man lay on the floor face down, his arms outflung. He was dead.

Beside the body, a little boy was squatting. He was no more than seven or eight, with dark hair just like the hair of the dead man. With one pudgy hand he was clutching the dead man's coat, and with the other he was holding a huge revolver which was so heavy that he could barely lift it. He was dry-eyed, but his youthful little face was tight and defiant.

HE PUT the heavy gun down on the floor when he saw the three white men in the doorway. Tears suddenly came streaming down his face.

"They—k-killed my dad!" he gulped. "Those J-Japs—killed my dad. They shot through the door!"

Johnny Kerrigan knelt beside the youngster, put an arm about his thin shoulders.

"Poor kid!" he said softly.

The boy held on tight with one hand to his dead father's coat. He looked up at Johnny. "Are you the men who were coming to meet him? Kerrigan and Murdoch and Klaw?"

Johnny nodded. "That's right, sonny. But the Japs got him first. I'm sorry, kid."

"What's your name, sonny?" Steve Klaw asked gently.

"Tony," said the boy. "Tony Balbo." He looked from one to the other of them. "Did—did you kill all those Japs who killed Dad? Did you?"

Steve nodded. "We paid off, Tony—in part. We'll pay off plenty more before we're through."

Johnny Kerrigan lifted the lad to his feet. "Come on, Tony. We've got to get you out of here. We'll have to leave your dad here till later."

The boy was sobbing as he stood up and fumbled with one hand under his blouse. He brought out a soiled scrap of paper, which he handed to Steve, together with three sheets of well-thumbed onion-skin.

"My dad wrote this when he looked out the window and saw that the Japs had the house surrounded. He told me, if anything happened to him, to give it to you with these diagrams."

Stephen Klaw took the papers. The three onion-skin sheets contained diagrams which were quite evidently charts of aeroplane flights, with maps of the territory covered. The other contained a hasty pencil scrawl.

Dan Murdoch, looking at the charts, exclaimed, "If those aren't the plans for projected air-raids on this city, I'll eat them!"

Stephen Klaw was already reading the hasty pencil scrawl on the fourth sheet:

To the F.B.I.—

These are the Japanese plans for tonight. The hour is some time before dawn. God knows if I'll ever get these to you—it looks like they've got me. I'll never live till your three men get here. But I can still die trying to do my bit for the country that adopted me and gave me a chance to bring up my son. There are a thousand Japs circulating in this section of town—you can't tell them from Filipinos. They're all set for a big blow at the city when they get a signal. I don't know what the signal is, but the person who will give the signal is a woman. Her name is Madam Setti, but she goes by other names, too. You'll know her by the little red "S" tattooed on her left shoulder. She was once a geisha girl in Yokohama, and that's her mark. Look out for her. She's the most dangerous woman in the world.

STEPHEN KLAW gave the note to Kerrigan and Murdoch. While they read it, he went to the window which looked out on the back yard. He pulled aside the blind, which was tightly drawn, and peered into the night.

From far below, a shot sounded, and a bullet gouged into the lintel, less than a foot from his face.

Steve grimaced, but he did not back at once. He looked out to the west, where the sky was a deep crimson from the reflection of the conflagration along the river front. Those fires out there had been set with devilish cunning. They had spread so fast and furiously that it was taking the combined efforts of the fire and police departments to fight them. The rest of the city was left under the care of the air raid wardens and the auxiliary firemen, who had not yet been equipped with fire apparatus. In the event of a raid, or of sabotage in some other part of town, the result would be incalculably disastrous.

A second shot blasted from below, and the slug almost grazed Steve's ear. He stepped away from the window this time.

Kerrigan and Murdoch had laid the body of Manuel Balbo on the couch. Murdoch took the tablecloth off the table, and covered him with it. He turned to little Tony, who had taken hold of Johnny Kerrigan's hand.

"Your father was a brave man, Tony," he said. "You can always be proud of him."

Tony's eyes were fixed upon the still shape. "I'll be p-proud," he whispered through his tears. "Always!"

Then he turned, still holding tightly to Johnny Kerrigan's hand, and allowed himself to be led out into the hall.

CHAPTER 2
"SEE YOU IN HELL!"

STEVE KLAW had already stepped out into the corridor, picking his way among the bodies. It was he who, looking up toward the skylight, spotted the men with the blowguns, outlined against the sky above.

The gun in his hand jerked twice as he blasted at those dim shapes. One of them disappeared from the opening, while the other toppled down to land at Steve's feet.

Almost at once, other figures appeared up there, with guns. They must have thought to take the three silently, by surprise, as they came out of the room. But now that the element of surprise was gone, they preferred, apparently, to attack with guns.

Slugs smashed down into the hall, burying themselves in the bodies that lay there. But now, Stephen Klaw was no longer alone. Murdoch had leaped out beside him; and Johnny Kerrigan, thrusting little Tony back into the room, sprang out to join them.

Together, the three G-men blasted at those attackers on the roof, and once more the old house shook with the thunder of gunfire.

Another body came toppling down, and the attackers withdrew their heads. But they continued to snipe from a few feet back of the skylight opening, sending their shots into the front part of the hall, so that it would be impossible for the three to reach the head of the stairs.

Kerrigan, Murdoch and Klaw backed up into the room where Manuel Balbo's body lay. They looked at each other, then at little Tony. The same unspoken thought was in the minds of all three: whatever chances they might be willing to take for themselves, they must not expose the boy to further danger.

"We've got to clear the roof!" said Dan Murdoch. "We can't take the kid out through the street anyway—not with that mob waiting out there."

Johnny Kerrigan put his hand on Steve's shoulder. "You stay here with Tony, Shrimp. Dan and I will rush the roof. Then you and the kid follow."

"You can't make it," Steve said. "They'll cut you down!"

Murdoch shrugged. "They can't do more than kill us once for trying."

"Wait a minute!" Steve exclaimed. He switched off the light, and went over to the window. He pulled the blind aside.

"There's a fire escape here," he said over his shoulder. "The Japs are in the yard below, but they

can't see up here with the light out. We can make it to the roof by the ladder, and take those birds up above in the flank."

"Nice thinking, Shrimp," Dan said. "Let's go—"

He stopped abruptly, as Steve raised a hand for silence.

"Some one's coming down the ladder!" Steve whispered. "The Japs had the same idea. They figure on taking us in the rear!"

As he spoke, he was slipping new clips into his automatics. Out in the hall, the sporadic shooting was still continuing. Johnny Kerrigan, standing in the doorway, was sending an occasional shot up into the skylight, to discourage the attackers from coming too close to the opening. Down below, the shouts of the angry mob were rising. They were getting up enough courage to storm the house now.

Klaw held the blind aside, his automatic ready, as the ghostly shapes came down the fire escape ladder from the roof. Within the room, the darkness was thick and silent. The only sound was the swift breathing of little Tony Balbo. Even the firing from the skylight had ceased, and the roar of the mob in the street was reduced to a dull and ominous grumble. It was as if they were all waiting for the result of this flank attack from the direction of the fire escape.

In the dark, Dan Murdoch stood at the doorway, watching the skylight. Klaw remained at the window, his eyes on the fire escape. Johnny Kerrigan thrust little Tony into a far corner, and then moved over into the center of the room. He cocked both his revolvers.

"All right, Steve," he said. "I have the window covered. Any time you're ready."

"Right! Another minute. There's a couple of them on the fire escape. Two or three more coming down. One machine-gun." HE KEPT his eye glued to the crack, holding the shade with one hand. Then he said abruptly: "Here goes."

He gave the shade a yank and sent it rattling upward, exposing the window. At the same time he swung to one side, out of Kerrigan's line of fire. He raised both his automatics, and began to pump shots through the glass. The pane shattered as both he and Johnny Kerrigan sent a hail of lead into the huddled group on the fire escape landing. The machine-gun out there began to stutter, and then became silent. A man screamed. A shadowy figure threw up its arms and went hurtling through the railing.

Simultaneously, Dan Murdoch began to shoot at the skylight, where the attackers had once more appeared. Bullets came smashing down from above, to gouge the floor at Murdoch's feet; but he stood there calmly, pumping shot after shot up into the opening.

The room reverberated with the continuous detonations, and the air became acrid with smoke. More men were streaming down the fire escape ladder to the attack, and the pile of bodies on the landing became high. But still they came, those little yellow men, grimly intent upon finishing these three. Klaw emptied one gun, and stopped to reload while Kerrigan covered him; then Klaw covered while Kerrigan loaded. But in the doorway, Murdoch had no one to spell him. His guns were empty, and a gruesome pile of dead lay almost at his feet. Now, as he reloaded swiftly, the attackers began to drop through the skylight. Two or three landed on the soft carpet of bodies which covered the floor before Murdoch could slip fresh shells into his weapon. He hurled the empty gun at the foremost of the attackers, hit him squarely in the face. Then he threw himself at the man and sent him careening back into his fellows.

Murdoch scrambled on the floor, searching the bodies there, until he found a revolver. He didn't know if it was loaded, but he raised it and fired into the seething mass above him. The gun bucked and roared as he pulled the trigger again and again, and the killers fell.

Directly above him, he saw other figures leaping down from the skylight into the battle, blasting away with their guns as they jumped. One of them landed alongside Murdoch, and thrust the muzzle of a gun against his ribs. This was the last of the attackers from the skylight. There were no more coming through. But one single shot from his gun would finish Murdoch as efficiently as a dozen. The firing inside was hot and heavy, and Dan knew that Kerrigan and Klaw must be hard-pressed, else one of them would have swung to his assistance by this time. He refused to call to them for help. He smashed a fist into his shadowy attacker's face, expecting at the same time to feel the driving impact of a slug in his ribs.

But the shot did not come. Instead, the man opened up his mouth and yelled, jerking away quickly. Murdoch's fist crashed into the man's face, and the fellow tripped against something directly behind him, and went over backward.

Tony Balbo's face was a white blob in the darkness, close to the floor. He peered up at Dan. "I bit him in the leg!" he said proudly. "It made him yell, and when you hit him, he tripped over me!"

Murdoch grinned broadly. "Good kid, Tony. You saved my life!"

The firing inside the room ceased suddenly, and Murdoch pulled little Tony in there. Kerrigan and Klaw were reloading their guns, grinning. Outside the window, there was a litter of dead bodies.

"We kind of discouraged them!" Johnny Kerrigan boomed.

The enemy had suffered frightful losses. Their dead lay thick in the hall and on the fire escape landing.

"They've either decided to give up," said Stephen Klaw, "or else they're reorganizing for another try."

He went to the window and pulled the blind down again. At the door, Dan Murdoch flipped the electric light switch. There was a click, but no light. The electric light bulb had been hit.

Johnny Kerrigan took out his flashlight and snapped it on. The beam of light sprayed across the room, and immediately there was a volley of shots from somewhere outside which smashed in through the blind.

Dan Murdoch swept little Tony Balbo out of the line of fire.

Klaw grinned. "It looks like they haven't given up."

"Personally," said Johnny Kerrigan, "I feel flattered. They're certainly throwing away a lot of man-power to get us."

"It's not us they want," Kerrigan grunted. His eyes swung to little Tony. "It's the message his dad left for us."

Now, the murmur of the mob rose in a rumbling roar of hatred from the street below. They heard the sound of crashing glass, and then there was a multitude of footsteps on the stairs, rushing upward in a charge of fury.

"Well, mopes," said Stephen Klaw, "this looks like it. How many rounds have you guys got left?"

Dan Murdoch grinned sheepishly and spread his empty hands. "I haven't got a gun," he said.

Johnny Kerrigan pulled a handful of loose cartridges out

of his pocket, began stuffing them into the chambers of his revolvers.

"I have nine shells left," he said.

Klaw hefted his automatics. "I have one full clip, and three shots left in the other."

Dan Murdoch took the flashlight from Johnny Kerrigan, and darted out into the hall. He pawed around on the floor and came up with two revolvers, which had belonged to the attacking Japs. He broke them, squinted into the chambers, and nodded.

"Both almost full," he said. "I guess we can take a few of these punks with us!"

ALL THREE of them turned to look at little Tony Balbo. It was he that they were really worried about. As for themselves, they had long ago calculated that they were living on borrowed time, enjoying lives which they had forfeited many times in the past. Not for nothing were they known as the Suicide Squad. In the F.B.I. they never received a routine assignment, but were always held in reserve for those jobs for which the Director would ordinarily hesitate to ask for volunteers. They rated those missions from which it was not expected that they would return alive.

Originally, there had been five of them on the Suicide Squad, then four, now three. Every day that they went out on a new assignment, there was always the expectation that tomorrow there would be only two, or one—or none. But thus far, Death had seemed to be avoiding them—if only for the reason that they appeared to be seeking it. The legend of the Suicide Squad had grown to huge proportions among those legions of spies and saboteurs who worked for the enemies of America. Some said that the Suicide Squad was indestructible; others that they were lucky fighting fools who had gotten by thus far only because there is a special god who looks after madmen.

Nevertheless, the secret agents of the Axis in America had developed a healthy respect for the Suicide Squad—which accounted for the elaborate trap in which Kerrigan, Murdoch and Klaw now found themselves.

But they would not have had it otherwise. They were a trio of reckless, fighting hellions, with no regard for the value of their own lives. They lived only for today, and for the privilege of standing side by side in a battle where the odds were high against them. In that they gloried, and in that lay the reason for the fear in which they were held by their enemies.

But now it was different. Alone, these three might have rejoiced in the heavy odds they faced. That they had come unscathed through the attack they had just sustained, would have meant to them only that they had another chance to risk their lives. But now they had to consider the fact that a child's life was in their hands—plus the information contained in Manuel Balbo's message.

The house was rocking to the rushing feet of the mob. In another couple of minutes, the first of them would reach the top.

"All right, Steve," said Johnny Kerrigan. "Dan and I will stay here and serve them tea. You take Tony and try to make it down the fire escape. I doubt if you get through. But there's nothing else for it."

Klaw nodded somberly. There was nothing that any of them

would have have wanted more at this moment than to stand shoulder to shoulder, and to go down together, taking as many of their enemies with them as they could. But they realized that their duty demanded that they at least make the attempt to get Tony and the message through.

Klaw said, "See you in hell, mopes."

"See you in hell, Shrimp!"

Steve Klaw took Tony by the hand and turned toward the window.

CHAPTER 3
BLACKOUT

THE FIRST of the howling mob were already at the top landing. Kerrigan sprang to the doorway and sent three swift shots into the darkness. That stopped them for a moment.

"Get going, Shrimp!" Johnny called over his shoulder.

Out in the hallway there was a mingling of raucous yells as those behind urged the others up the stairs. But above that shouting, a new noise was heard—the creaking of a door.

Steve Klaw, already at the window, stopped short, with little Tony at his side. He swung around. That creaking had come from this room!

Both Murdoch and Kerrigan had heard it, too. Kerrigan slammed the corridor door shut, and turned around. All three of them stared at the wall of the room, where a panel was sliding open.

A woman stood revealed in that secret doorway.

She was a tall woman, with dark hair coiled high on her head. She wore a black gown, unrelieved except for a gleaming belt of silver around her narrow waist. Her face was thin and her eyes black, and she had a queer complexion which was neither white nor yellow, but which might have been classed as Eurasian.

She stood there in the doorway for a moment, completely at ease, completely poised, as if she had just come from a dinner party. Her eyes studied them as if she wished to engrave their faces indelibly upon her memory.

"Follow me," she said. "I can show you a way out!"

The mob was grumbling out in the hall, getting up its courage for a rush upon the closed door. But Kerrigan, Murdoch and Klaw paid it not the least attention. Their eyes were fixed on the woman.

"Who are you?" Stephen Klaw demanded.

She gave him a faint smile. "Does a name mean so much? When your lives are at stake, do you stop to ask whose help you are getting?"

There was just the faintest trace of accent in her speech; enough to brand her as foreign, but not sufficient to identify the country of her origin.

"Come quickly!" she urged. "If you wait, the mob will tear you apart!"

Johnny Kerrigan grinned. "Lady, we appreciate your interest. But we'd like to know which side you're on."

She stirred impatiently. "You fools! Do you think I'd show you this way out if I didn't want to help you?"

"Maybe," said Johnny. "Maybe you'd like to know what Manuel Balbo told us before he died."

Her black eyes flickered. "Did you find him—alive?"

Johnny chuckled. "We got a message from him, if that's what you want to know."

There was a pounding of feet out in the hall, accompanied by wild shouts. The crowd was rushing the door.

Dan Murdoch yanked the door open. A compact mass of armed men was within half a dozen feet of the room, leaping over the dead bodies of the Japs.

Kerrigan turned his gun on the mob, and emptied it into them. The crowd recoiled, then turned and fled. They reached the head of the stairs, but could not descend, because of the press of men behind them.

He slammed the door shut again.

"It's no use killing them," he said. "They have plenty more men. That's no haphazard mob. It's led by professional killers!"

"And," said the woman in the doorway, "you can't have much ammunition left. I advise you to come with me."

"You haven't told us your name yet," Steve reminded her.

She shrugged. "Call me Madam X, if you must have a name. And now, for the last time, will you come?" Her eyes swept to little Tony, who was pressing against Stephen Klaw. "Even if you don't care about yourselves, you have a boy there. Do you want him to perish too?"

That decided them. Steve glanced at Kerrigan and Murdoch. "What say, boys?"

"Why not?" Murdoch said. "The lady seems to be nicer company than that mob of howling fanatics outside."

"Thank you," said the woman. "This way!"

SHE TURNED and disappeared into the dark passage, and Steve Klaw stepped through after her.

"Watch this, mopes," he said over his shoulder. "Keep Tony between us. Who ever this dame is, I don't like her!"

Tony plucked at Steve's sleeve. "It's Madam Setti!" he whispered. "It's the woman my father was afraid of. I never saw her, but I'm sure!"

Johnny Kerrigan said, "This ought to be fun. Let's go!"

He pushed Tony ahead of him, after Steve, into the passage. Dan Murdoch waited only to send the last of his bullets through the already riddled door, with the idea of discouraging the mob for a few moments more. Then he followed the others.

The passage led down a steep bank of stairs. No sooner had Dan Murdoch stepped through, than the panel began to close. The woman, somewhere below, must have pressed a hidden switch which controlled the door. The stairs and the passage were thrown into absolute darkness.

Kerrigan produced his flashlight, and sent a beam lancing downward. It disclosed the woman, almost at the foot of the stairs, with Stephen Klaw right behind her, so close to her that he could reach out and seize her at the first display of treachery.

The woman waited till they had all joined her on the narrow landing. It seemed that there was only a blank wall here, but she pressed another button somewhere, and the wall swung away, revealing another passage, this one level. From its location, they judged that it led into the adjoining house.

They followed the woman through it, into a bare room, devoid of all furniture. She led them across, and opened a door into the hall.

"There you are," she said. "We're in the building next door. You can get out through the front door. They won't even be looking for you out there. They think you're still trapped in Balbo's room."

"Is this where you live?" Johnny Kerrigan asked as he looked around the empty room.

"I—live across the hall," she said, after a moment's hesitation. She pointed to the door of one of the flats.

"H'm." Stephen Klaw looked her up and down. "You must be the best-dressed girl in the neighborhood."

"I just came home from a party," she told him. "I heard people talking in the street, and when I realized that you were trapped in the house next door, I remembered the secret passage."

"Wonderful!" said Dan Murdoch. "Isn't it remarkable that there should just happen to be a secret passage into that flat where we were?"

"Don't be a fool!" she said impatiently. "These houses are honeycombed with secret passages. They were built by bootleg gangs, twenty years ago. They've been unused for years, but everyone in the neighborhood knows about them." She gestured imperiously toward the stairs leading to the street. "Hurry! You still have time to escape with the boy before the mob realizes you're in here. Why don't you go?"

Steve Klaw's eyes locked with hers. "What about a look at your left shoulder blade, lady?" he asked.

She flushed. "What—what do you mean?"

"He means he wants to see if you have an S tattooed there," Johnny Kerrigan explained.

"I don't understand. If this is a joke, I think it's in poor taste. If this is your way of showing your gratitude for being given a way of escape, then you are not American gentlemen!"

"All right!" Steve Klaw said swiftly. "You win. But the next time we meet, I'm going to get a look at your left shoulder!

He took little Tony's hand and started for the stairs.

The woman smiled. "Till the next time we meet then, Mr. G-man."

She turned and went to the door of the apartment which she had indicated as her own.

"Good-by!" she said softly, and went into the room.

TONY PLUCKED at Steve Klaw's sleeve. "I'm afraid of that woman!" he whispered.

Klaw nodded. He glanced at Kerrigan and Murdoch. "What say, mopes?"

Murdoch's eyes were glistening in the semi-gloom. "I say she's got something cute figured out for us. She didn't do this out of friendship!"

"Right," Johnny said. "It looks to me like it might be a trick to get us out in the open. They don't know how short of ammunition we were. Maybe they figure it'll take too many more lives to get us, barricaded in that room. So they want us out in the street, where they can really cut us down."

Klaw said. "If they want us in the street, we'll go the other way."

Treading on tiptoe, he moved down the hall, toward the stairs which led to the roof. Through the flimsy partitions they could hear the shouting of the mob in the adjoining house, as it vented its rage and disappointment at finding its quarry gone.

Silently, the three made their way upward, with little Tony sticking close to Steve. At the top floor, they saw that the skylight was properly closed, as it should be in any self-respecting house.

"Those birds didn't come from this house," Dan Murdoch whispered.

Steve shook his head. "They must have come from Number Nineteen. That's where the first blowgun artist made his attack from. Take it easy now. There'll still be some of them on the roofs!"

"I'll check," said Johnny.

Steve handed him one of the automatics with a full clip, and Kerrigan climbed the ladder. He pushed the skylight open, and stuck his head out. Then he climbed up on the roof, being careful not to raise himself too high. After a moment, he stuck his head over the edge of the skylight. "Come on up!" he called softly.

They sent Tony first. Then Murdoch went, and Steve Klaw followed him. On the roof, they all crouched low.

A great red haze suffused the sky, and off to the west a mass of spurting flame and smoke formed a holocaust of conflagration. The fire at the river was out of control, apparently. Long, pale anti-aircraft lights probed into the sky from searchlight batteries, criss-crossing the firmament with their sensitive, probing fingers.

From the house next door, which they had quit, there emanated the wild cries of the bloodthirsty mob.

Quietly, Johnny Kerrigan led the way across the roof, in the opposite direction. He chuckled. "They certainly aren't expecting us up this way," he whispered. "They've withdrawn all their men from the roofs."

They worked over toward the front of the house, and peered over the cornice.

"The street lights are all out!" Dan Murdoch exclaimed.

"It's a blackout!" said Steve Klaw. He flung up an arm and pointed at the tall skyscrapers—gigantic ghosts to the south. There was not a light showing in any of them.

"The Japs are trying an air raid at last!" said Johnny Kerrigan. "This must be their zero hour!"

"Let's be going!" Dan Murdoch instructed. "It looks like we might be too late with our information already!"

THE OFFICE of the First Interceptor Command was an inspiring picture of disciplined activity. As Dan Murdoch followed the orderly past the huge glass-enclosed Plotting Room, he saw the well-trained group of men and women volunteers at the Chart Table, with earphones on their heads. Occasionally, one of them would lean over the huge chart of the Northeastern Seaboard which occupied the entire table, and place a little colored marker with an arrow at a certain spot, in his or her assigned sector. Then another operator would place another arrow in an adjoining sector. At the same time, a man at a great blackboard at one side of the room would put down certain figures. Thus was plotted the position, direction, rate of speed and numbers of any unidentified airplanes within a five hundred miles radius.

Upstairs in the Staff Room to which Dan Murdoch was taken, a group of officers watched through glass windows every notation that was made in the chart room below, with protractors hovering above the scale maps spread out before them.

Major Flanagan, who was in charge of the staff, was pacing up and down beside his desk, keeping an eye on every one of the scale maps. He greeted Dan Murdoch warmly.

"How are you, Dan? Your Chief phoned me that you had contacted Balbo, and found him dead. But you got something there, anyway?"

Murdoch nodded. He handed over the onion-skin tracings.

"Johnny Kerrigan took Tony Balbo back to F.B.I. headquarters," he said.

"Steve Klaw remained back there outside Number Thirteen, watching the mob. He figured he might get a line on what's being planned."

The major spread the papers on his desk. His brow wrinkled as he studied them. "You've looked at these, Dan?" he asked.

"I have, sir." Murdoch, an ex-Marine aviator himself, knew how to read a chart as well as anyone. "There are three charts there. One covers Long Island, another Westchester, and the third is a chart of Western Connecticut. There are directional lines on each of them, indicating three possible channels for air raids, all converging on New York."

"Yes, I see," said Flanagan. "But look here, Dan—" he put his finger on the Westchester map—"the course of the planes as marked here seems to indicate that the inception point of the projected raid lies somewhere west of Poughkeepsie! *It means that their planes will take off from within the United States!*"

"Yes, sir," said Murdoch. "And the others are similar. The Connecticut map shows the inception of the attacking flight as being east of Hartford, while this Long Island map places the take-off near Patchogue."

"By God," said Major Flanagan, "these maps must be a hoax. All three of those points are within the jurisdiction of the First Interceptor Command, and I can personally vouch for the fact that there isn't a possibility of a hangar or a field from which they could take off, at any of those places. We've covered the countryside with a fine-tooth comb. I can tell you definitely that there are no planes hidden anywhere within five hundred miles of the city!"

MURDOCH NODDED somberly. "I'm sure you're right, sir. Yet I swear that an attack is going to be made along these lines."

"But how, man?"

Murdoch shrugged. "That's what we've got to find out."

Major Flanagan said earnestly, "We know that the enemy have scheduled an attack for some time before dawn tomorrow. It may be tonight, it may not be till dawn actually breaks. But in any event, we have night patrols scouting a thousand miles at sea. The Third and Fifth Destroyer Squadron are covering the sea approaches, using the most sensitive sound detectors ever built. We have two aircraft carriers supplementing the land-based patrols, and the carriers are accompanied by a full complement of cruisers and destroyers. I'll stake my life that it's virtually impossible for an attacking plane to reach the shores of the eastern seaboard tonight!"

Dan Murdoch bent over the maps.

While he studied them, Major Flanagan picked up his phones and issued swift orders for extra precautions to be taken in the neighborhood of the three points indicated on the maps.

He hung up, and turned to Murdoch. "If there are any hidden planes that we might have overlooked they'll be found now. But I'm sure there aren't!"

"And yet," Murdoch said thoughtfully, "there must be some explanation of these maps. Manuel Balbo knew what he was doing."

"Then the danger threatens in some way that we can't guess," Major Flanagan said. "It's up to us to find it out. Quick!"

Murdoch said, "I think I'll be going back to Steve. I'm sure the answer lies in that section."

"For God's sake, work fast!" Flanagan begged. "They may strike between now and dawn—any time."

"I'll do my best, sir," Murdoch said. "And so will Johnny and Steve."

"I'll give you a hundred men if you want them," Flanagan said. "A thousand. We'll mop up that whole section—"

Murdoch smiled wryly. "And most likely miss the devils who are planning this," he said. "There are thousands of innocent people in that section, as good Americans as you or I. They're the ones who'd be caught in a round-up, while the real conspirators would be clever enough to elude the net." He paused, a faraway look in his eyes. "I think our way is better. I have a hunch that Steve has his eye on the answer right now."

CHAPTER 4
THE DIVA-KING

IN THE darkness of the blacked-out city, Stephen Klaw stood at the curb, directly opposite Number Thirteen, watching the milling mob in the street. He had arranged with Dan and Johnny to contact him back here after they had completed their errands, then he had worked his way around to the front of Number Thirteen.

The mob still raged frenziedly inside that house, and none of them thought for a moment to look for their quarry almost in their midst.

The great fire at the docks cast an eerie glow over the whole city, and Steve thought wryly that if enemy bombers were seeking the city, that conflagration would guide them like a beacon, in spite of the blackout. This thing had been planned very thoroughly, with devilish attention paid to detail.

Steve had his two automatics back, for Kerrigan hadn't needed a gun once he was out of the district; he had promised to bring more ammunition when he returned.

Steve lit a cigarette, and watched the small group who emerged from the house next to Number Thirteen. Immediately, he stiffened.

There were four people in that group. One of them was the woman who had given the name of Madam X. She had a fur coat on now. Two of the men with her were of ordinary stature; one was fair-haired, with distinctly Teutonic features, while the other was a little shorter, and very dark. But it was the third man who drew Klaw's attention.

This one was built on gigantic proportions. He was so huge that he made the two men and the woman look like pigmies. This massive giant wore only a pair of trousers and a thin, short-sleeved shirt. The man's face was a dreadful gargoyle as he walked through the shrieking, screaming mob in front of Number Thirteen.

As soon as the frenzied mob spotted him, all sound ceased. A dreadful and a terrified silence descended upon them, and they moved back to make way for him.

He spoke, looking contemptuously over their heads. His voice was a deep, rumbling bass, which seemed to emanate from the very bowels of the earth. His words were in a strange and foreign tongue, and they seemed to strike like lashes at the men who appeared to be the leaders of the mob.

They looked at him blankly, apparently not comprehending what he said, but understanding that he was frightfully angry with them.

When he ceased talking, there was utter silence, and the men in the mob turned to the woman, questioningly. She spoke to them in English:

"The Diva-God is angry with you," she interpreted. "He says that you have earned death a thousand times, by letting those three Americans escape. You left the roofs unguarded, and they escaped. He is angry with me—I, too, have earned death. But he needs me yet awhile. You twelve, he does not need. You must pay now for your foolishness. Now!"

THE REST of the mob had slunk away into the night, leaving only the giant with his three companions, and those twelve miserable wretches.

Across the street, Stephen Klaw had melted into the shadows of a doorway, from where he watched the scene. The woman's words had struck deeply into the chords of his memory. Years ago, before ever he had thought of being a G-man, he had been a soldier of fortune. One of his jobs had been a confidential mission for Chiang-Kai-shek, in Korea, and it was there that he had first met Dan Murdoch, who was then a Marine aviator on duty with the American consul at Keijo, the Korean capital. And, in company with Murdoch, he had visited Shaman temples where they had seen the gigantic statues of the weirdly ugly Diva-God, who guarded the entrance of each temple.

The woman had called this giant the Diva-God!

Things clicked into order in Steve's brain. He understood now, the hold which the Imperial Devil of Nippon had upon these poor fools here in America. He understood, too, the reckless fanaticism with which they had thrown away their lives upstairs in Number Thirteen. The answer was Shamanism—a religion of fear and utter, abject slavery. The fools looked upon this giant as the earthly incarnation of their god of the old country!

Stephen Klaw was treated to an object lesson in the power of this oriental religion over its disciples.

The twelve miserable fools threw themselves upon their knees before the giant. In the hand of each there appeared a gun.

The giant uttered a single word, and twelve guns were raised to twelve temples. The giant spoke another word, and twelve triggers were pulled, as if by a single finger. The twelve shots blended into one, and the next moment, a dozen still figures lay in the street.

The giant grunted. Then he spoke over his shoulder to the woman and two men, and started to walk slowly down the street.

Stephen Klaw had both his guns out; he could have shot that giant easily from where he stood. But he refrained from doing so.

To kill that so-called Diva-God would not remove the threat which lay over the city. There was no doubt that the air raid planned for tonight would proceed along its pre-determined lines, whether the Diva-God were killed or not. The only chance of preventing that raid lay in following these people.

Steve kept in the shadows as much as he could. They walked purposefully, those four, with swift strides, as if they had a definite task to accomplish. The woman and the two men almost had to run to keep up with the giant. As if by magic, the street was completely deserted now; it looked no different from any other in the city under blackout conditions.

Steve stopped short in the shadow of a doorway, as the four abruptly started to cross the street in the middle of the block. He was a little behind them, and they did not even turn to see if they were followed. He saw now where they were heading.

There was a long limousine parked down the street. The fair-haired man got in under the wheel, and the other man held the door for the giant and the woman. Then the other man got in, and the car moved away.

Stephen Klaw cursed. His only chance of following them meant reaching that car. He was setting himself for a running leap at the car which would have to pass him when he saw the other car swing into the block. Like the limousine, its headlights were out, but a flashlight blinked three times inside that car.

Steve grinned, let out a sigh of relief, and allowed the limousine to pass him.

Almost at once, the second car pulled up; the door swung open. Steve jumped inside. Johnny Kerrigan was at the wheel, and Dan Murdoch sat beside him.

Klaw snapped, "Keep after that limousine, Johnny. Don't lose it!"

THE LIMOUSINE was now only a dim shape in the night, far up the street. It was turning the corner. Johnny pulled after it, going just fast enough to keep it in sight.

Swiftly, Stephen Klaw told Murdoch and Kerrigan what had happened. When he finished, he demanded, "How do you two mopes happen to be together?"

"I picked Dan up, around the corner," Johnny explained. "I took Tony Balbo to the Field Office, but there wasn't a soul there except a night man on duty at the telephone. Every available man is out at the river front. I hated to leave the kid there, with only one man to watch him, but there was nothing else to do."

"It would be just too bad if anything happened to Tony," Steve said. "The F.B.I. pledged its word that Tony would be taken care of, if Manuel Balbo got killed. The honor of the F.B.I. is at stake—not to mention that kid's life."

"That kid saved my life tonight," Dan Murdoch said.

"What about the Filipino girl who tipped you off to Balbo, Steve?" Kerrigan asked. "What happened to her?"

"Maria Flores?" Steve said. "I don't know. I'm worried about her. She disappeared right after I talked to her."

The limousine had made two or three turns, moving at a snail-like pace through the black, deserted streets. Now it came to a stop before a low, one-storied building which had at one time been a motion picture theatre but which, from its dilapidated appearance, must have been condemned and closed for years.

Kerrigan coasted to a stop, a hundred yards behind the limousine.

The giant, the woman, and the two men descended from the car, and headed swiftly for the boarded-up entrance of the old theatre.

"What the hell?" exclaimed Johnny. "It looks like they intend to walk through those boards!"

But they didn't. The group stopped in front of a sidewalk elevator lift, at one side of the entrance. The woman pressed a button, and the covers of the lift began to rise. When it was fully opened, all four of them stepped on to the platform, and it began to descend. The lift cover closed over them.

From a bag at his feet Kerrigan extracted a dozen of the new D-42 high-explosive grenades, which had passed army tests, but which had not yet gone into mass production. These D-42s were no larger than a medium-sized lime, but they contained the newly-developed thermo-toluene explosive, which gave them the same demolition power as a twenty-five pound bomb. He gave some to Dan and Steve, and pocketed a few himself. Then he produced fresh clips for Steve's automatics.

"Let's go!" he said.

The three of them walked swiftly, surveying the somber and time-wracked exterior of the theatre.

Dan Murdoch found the button which they had seen the woman press. Immediately, the lift cover began to rise. The platform came to the surface, stopped.

The three G-men looked at each other.

"Here goes nothing!" said Klaw. Kerrigan and Murdoch followed him onto the platform. Murdoch reached over and pressed the button again, and the lift began to descend. The cover closed over them, enveloping them in a black void....

CHAPTER 5
ATTACK!

IN A small room within the old theatre, a man sat at a long control panel. He was a thin man, with a sharp nose and a red gash of a mouth, and wide-spaced eyes which denoted a high order of intelligence.

A multitude of gadgets decorated the panel before which he sat. Directly in front of the man was a large television screen, which was blank at the moment. The man's eyes were riveted upon the electric clock on the wall, which showed fourteen minutes before midnight.

A buzzer sounded at his elbow, and he pressed a button in response. Immediately, the door of the room opened. The woman—Madam X—entered, followed by the huge giant whom she had called the Diva-God.

The narrow-eyed man arose from the control panel, clicked his heels, and bowed with military brusqueness.

"Good evening, Madam Setti," he said.

"Good evening, *Herr* Captain von Berner," she replied. She waved a careless hand at the giant behind her. "This is our Diva-God. I don't believe you have met him before."

The giant was no longer as arrogant as he had appeared in front of Number Thirteen.

"How do you do, von Berner," he said, in careful, precise German. "It is a pleasure to speak my own language again. For ten weeks I have acted the part of that damned Diva-God, for the benefit of witless fools!" He bowed from the waist, as von Berner had done. "I am Heinrich Kojan. You have heard of me?"

"Indeed, yes," said von Berner. "The strongest man in Germany. You acted as Himmler's aide until you were required to play the part of the Diva-God."

"Quite so," said Kojan. "As the representative of the Gestapo here, I take precedence in command over you, whenever I find it necessary. Please tell me what arrangements you have made."

Von Berner suppressed a frown. He answered in precise, military fashion. "The attack is set for midnight. As you see, it lacks twelve minutes of the zero hour. At ten minutes before

64

midnight, the three stratosphere bombers will be somewhere over New York. Their great height will preclude any possibility of their finding the objectives they seek. But at exactly ten-minutes of twelve, the crews of the three planes will throw the switches which turn over the controls to me here. Our agents at the three points of contact have laid cable which will act as antennae for the initial contact, after which I will be able to control them by wireless. At the three fields to be bombed, other agents have erected a secret television apparatus, all within a twenty-mile radius of this point, which will enable me to see the objectives on this screen. I will be able to guide the planes unerringly to the targets. The crews will already have bailed out, and will take their assigned positions for sabotage work."

The giant Kojan nodded. "When the three main flying fields have been destroyed, the land-based planes now patroling will not be able to re-fuel. They will have to return when they exhaust their present fuel, and will be unable to take off again. Then, our bombers, which have long ago started from our carriers in mid-ocean, will be able to fly in, unopposed, before the Americans can bring fighters from other interceptor commands into this district."

"Exactly!" said von Berner. "By dawn, the city will be ours. Once we have wiped out the population by poison gas, and have established a beach-head here, our forces will be too overwhelming to be dislodged. We will march south to Washington, and by tomorrow we will have cut off the two main centers of America from the rest of the country!"

MADAM SETTI drew herself up proudly. "And I shall have contributed to the victory!"

Von Berner bowed. "In no small part, Madam."

"There is only one thing I regret," she said, frowning. "It is that those three—the Suicide Squad—escaped with the information that Manuel Balbo gave them. Of course, there will not be time for them to guess from those drawings, just what our plan is. But I should not have let them get away!"

"Be patient," said Heinrich Kojan. "Tomorrow, we will find them again. When I have established Gestapo headquarters in New York, those three will be our first—guests!"

"We must also get that boy, Tony Balbo. And the girl, Maria Flores!" Madam Setti said viciously. "It was the Flores girl who betrayed the plan to the G-men, and Balbo who gave them the charts. Balbo is dead, but we can take vengeance upon the boy—make him pay for what his father has done!"

Von Berner smiled. "The Balbo boy was brought to the F.B.I. office tonight, and left in charge of only one man. My men, acting on my orders, killed the watchman and brought the boy here. He is in the execution room now. And so is the girl, Maria Flores!"

Just then the buzzer sounded, and von Berner pushed the button. The door opened, and the fair-haired man who had accompanied the giant appeared, his face working with excitement.

"Those three G-men are coming down in the lift!" he exclaimed.

The woman started toward the door. "This will indeed be a

pleasure! Come, Falken!" She took the fair-haired man by the arm. "We shall set the stage for them!"

Just then, a muted bell tinkled on the control board. Von Berner uttered an exclamation of excitement, and turned to the dials. He worked several of the gadgets, speaking into the tube as he did so. Hastily he adjusted earphones on his head, and began to operate the many controls.

Slowly, a picture materialized on the television screen—a picture of the interior of a huge bomber, with grim, hatchet-faced men at the controls.

"*I have them! I have them!*" von Berner shouted. "I've made contact with the bombers!"

He waved a hand at the woman. "Take care of those G-men, Madam Setti. *They must not reach this room!*"

"Don't worry," she said. "They won't!"

She nodded to Heinrich Kojan, and went out.

WHEN THE platform came to a stop, Kerrigan, Murdoch and Klaw stood tensely in the dark, waiting. Slowly, a door in front of them began to open. The brilliant light of the room into which it led almost blinded them for an instant.

"Get back, Shrimp," Johnny Kerrigan muttered. "Dan and I are going in first. You cover us."

Shoulder to shoulder, with guns in their hands, Murdoch and Kerrigan stepped out of the elevator and went into the lighted room.

It was a huge room, with a balcony running across the entire far side of it. And upon that balcony was the strangest tableau which a white man might ever have seen.

A man attired in a wide-sleeved Japanese robe stood with a huge two-edged sword gripped in both hands. Little Tony Balbo was lying, his neck stretched across a block at the robed man's feet, his dark hair held by another Jap. Just behind the platform, a man held the pretty Filipino girl, Maria Flores.

At the railing of the balcony, stood the woman, Madam Setti. She was smiling a crooked, twisted smile.

"You have come just in time!" she called down to Kerrigan and Murdoch. "You can witness two executions. These are the people whom you pledged your word to protect. Now you will watch them die!"

"Wait!" Kerrigan shouted. "You can't kill that kid!"

"Indeed we can!" said Madam Setti. "Unless you wish to buy his life, and the life of Maria Flores."

Dan Murdoch wet his lips. "What's the price?" he asked.

There was a light of evil triumph in the woman's eyes as she leaned over the railing. "Throw down your guns and surrender!" she spat at them. "Call your friend out from the elevator, and let him surrender, too. When you are my prisoners, I promise I will release the boy and the girl!"

Maria Flores twisted in the grip of her captor. "Don't believe her!" she screamed. "It's a lie. She'll torture you three, and kill Tony and me anyway—"

Her words were choked off by the hand of her captor as it clamped viciously across her mouth.

Madam Setti's face became livid with fury. She signaled and a door on the lower level was thrust open. A small horde of yellow men came charging into the room.

Kerrigan and Murdoch began to shoot, coolly, deliberately, at the leaders of that throng. From behind them, Stephen Klaw raised his automatic and sent one shot up on to the balcony. It caught the executioner in the chest, sent him hurtling back from the execution block, the broadsword flying from his grip. Then, without too much haste, Klaw took one of the thermo-toluene grenades from his pocket, pulled the pin, and hurled it over the heads of Kerrigan and Murdoch, into the attacking crowd on the main floor.

"Duck, guys!" he yelled, at his comrades.

Just as Kerrigan and Murdoch dropped to the floor, there was a terrific detonation, and metal scrap went flying in every direction. A pall of smoke arose about the massed attackers.

From prone positions on the floor, Kerrigan and Murdoch each threw one more of the grenades into that smoke-filled welter of death at the other end of the room, and dropped flat.

Klaw came out of the elevator shaft and joined them when they got to their feet. As the smoke began to fade, they saw more of the yellow men trying to get through, over the dead bodies.

Kerrigan, Murdoch and Klaw raced up the balcony stairs side by side, pumping shots ahead of them. Steve Klaw, who was on the outside, turned and sent a few well-placed shots into the crowd below, while Johnny and Dan continued to the top.

Then Steve turned and ran up to join them, and Murdoch dropped two more of the deadly grenades into the welter of killers below.

On the balcony, Madam Setti was lying across the railing, lifeless. There was a sliver of metal in her left temple, where a bomb splinter had caught her. The two Japs who had been holding Tony and Maria had turned to flee, but Kerrigan and Klaw cut them down before they could escape.

Kerrigan patted Tony on the shoulder. "Take it easy, kid," he said. "Everything's going to be all right!"

Maria Flores clung to Steve Klaw's arm. "I feel as if I'd been born again," she said. "I fully expected to die. But hurry. That giant—the Diva-God—is inside, with von Berner. I saw him when he went in!"

"Von Berner!" Dan Murdoch exclaimed. "Then this is their headquarters!"

With Tony and Maria in tow, they hurried down a long corridor. Behind them, a few survivors of the bombs were coming up the stairs.

Steve turned and let them have one more grenade, and that stopped them for good.

At the end of the corridor, there was a closed door. Before they were a dozen feet from it, the door opened, and the huge giant came out.

For a moment he stared unbelievingly at the three.

"*Himmel!*" he screamed. "They have come through!" He pounded on the door through which he had just come. "Lock yourself in, von Berner!" he shouted in German. "The three devils have got in here!"

Then he put his head down, and charged.

Johnny Kerrigan was in the lead. Grimly, he pointed his revolver at the huge giant and fired five times quickly, and with unerring accuracy.

The shots brought Heinrich Kojan up sharply, stopping him as if they had been a concrete ram. He swayed on his feet, took two steps more, then he pitched forward on his face.

STEPHEN KLAW had already leaped past him to the door. He heard von Berner on the other side, fumbling with the bolt, and he threw all his weight against it. The door gave under the impact, and Steve went sprawling inside, on hands and knees. He turned his head, and saw von Berner's twisted countenance.

"Damn you!" the man shrieked. He leveled his revolver at Steve and his finger tightened on the trigger.

From the hall came a single shot, and von Berner stiffened. A look of strange incredulity passed over his face, then was replaced by the blankness of death as he collapsed.

Stephen Klaw leaped to the television board.

On the screen, there was a huge stratosphere bomber, flying over an Interceptor Command Field. It was just going into a dive.

At his side he heard Dan Murdoch shout: "That's Mitchell Field! Stop that damned thing!"

Stephen Klaw twisted dials and pulled at switches with breathless haste. Still the bomber continued its dive. Dan Murdoch joined him, and they both kept twirling the controls haphazardly. Suddenly they saw the bomber go into a flat dive and burst into flames.

"Eureka!" shouted Steve, at the sight of the flaming ship.

"There must be other bombers like that, aiming for other fields," Murdoch said. "But without this television direction, they'll go astray. They'll probably dive in the ocean. I see the idea now, all right. They wanted to destroy our land-bases for the Interceptor Patrols. There must be a mass air attack on the way now!"

He turned around in search of a phone, saw that flames from outside were licking hungrily down the corridor. In a few moments the building would be completely gutted by flames.

"I think we better be going," said Johnny Kerrigan.

They couldn't get out the front, through the fire, but they found a back exit and made their way to the street. In the darkness they worked around to where they had left their car. They drove swiftly to the Office of the First Interceptor Command.

Major Flanagan was sitting tensely at his desk now, and the Plotting Room was humming with activity.

"We've spotted approaching planes, out at sea!" Flanagan told them. "It's suicide. Those planes can't possibly get through. Our fighters are taking off from all three Interceptor Fields. They'll be able to destroy every one of the bombers before they get within two hundred miles of the coast.

"I'm afraid though, that the enemy has planned some sabotage of the fields. If they did that, we'd he licked!"

Dan Murdoch grinned. "They planned it, all right, Major. But you don't have to worry. We sort of exploded their theory!"

He turned and winked at Tony and Maria, then looked at Steve Klaw and Johnny Kerrigan.

"I think," he said, "that a little drink would be in order."

Steve Klaw nodded. "We'll drink to the S on Madam Setti's shoulder, which we never saw."

He turned and put one hand on Tony's shoulder, the other on

Maria's. "And to a brave boy and girl." His eyes clouded. "Also, to the bravest father a boy ever had!"

There were tears in Tony Balbo's eyes as he looked up at Kerrigan, Murdoch and Klaw.

"We'll try to take his place, son, as best we can," Dan Murdoch whispered to the boy.

THE SUICIDE SQUAD
MEETS THE RISING SUN

CHAPTER 1
THE LOST LEGION

S TEPHEN KLAW knocked at the door of the Chief's office, and stepped inside. The Chief of the Federal Bureau of Investigation was on hands and knees behind his desk, searching for something on the floor.

"Good afternoon, sir," said Klaw. "You looking for something?"

The Chief raised his head. "I'm looking for nine thousand able-bodied Japanese men."

Steve raised his eyebrows. "The Japs must be shrinking these days!"

The Chief chuckled, and got to his feet, holding a small metal disk which he had picked up under the desk. "It rolled off the desk," he explained. "Come here, Steve. I sent for you, to look at this."

Steve came over and took the disk which the Chief handed to him. It was bright and shiny, made from some sort of cheap alloy. On one side of it there was a replica of the Rising Sun of Japan; on the other side, there was a series of Japanese characters, together with the number 2864 engraved in Roman numerals.

"Does it mean anything to you, Steve?"

The three G-men began to move
forward, shoulder to shoulder,
their guns blasting....

Klaw shook his head. "It looks like a military identification disk. Might be used by Japanese soldiers. But I can't read their damned language."

"I've had it translated," the Chief said grimly. "This particular bit of metal happens to be the identification disk of a lance corporal of the Imperial Nipponese Army."

"Was it sent home from Hawaii or some place?"

"No," the Chief said slowly. "It was found on the body of a Jap who shot himself. He was caught hiding inside a truck that had been wrecked in an accident on Highway 26, in Maryland. The driver of that truck was a white man, but that's all we can tell you about him, because he was burned beyond recognition. The truck was carrying a load of American made Browning rapid-fire rifles."

STEVE WHISTLED softly, but made no comment. The Chief went on, his voice incisive and grim. "Now let me give you the translation of the rest of the writing on this disk. See those characters engraved around the outer circle?"

"Yes, sir."

"Could you possibly guess what they say?"

"I wouldn't try, sir. The ways of the Tokyo Brethern are hard to guess."

"All right, I'll tell you. It says: *Imperial Nipponese Expeditionary Force in America!*"

"How nice of them," said Steve. "Maybe they've even got a Quisling picked out for us!"

"Perhaps, perhaps," the Chief said. "Although I don't think they'd find an American who'd take the job. But the point is,

Steve, that there does exist such an expeditionary force, based at some secret point within the United States. Very likely it's in the State of Maryland. They'd been here for years. They were planted here ten years ago, before we ever suspected that Japan was planning a Pearl Harbor. And what's more, I know the exact number of this so-called expeditionary force. It numbers nine thousand."

"Nine thousand, eh?" Klaw repeated. "That's what you were looking for under your desk."

"I'll tell you how we arrived at that figure, Steve. The last census shows that there were two hundred and forty-seven thousand Japanese aliens residing on the eastern seaboard last year. But *this* year, when all aliens were required to register, only two hundred and thirty-eight thousand complied. A check of the census shows that the nine thousand who failed to register—and who cannot be located—are all able-bodied men, between twenty-five and forty!"

He paused, and then asked slowly, "Can you imagine what catastrophes could be caused here by a well-trained, well-armed force of nine thousand men, operating from a secret base?"

Stephen Klaw slowly lit a cigarette. "Any clues as to the location of this secret base?"

"None at all. We know definitely, though, that arms and ammunition have been diverted from several large defense plants—stolen, in plain English—and shipped by truck into the base. The Jap who killed himself when caught, was in the act of transporting six crates of the Brownings, with enough ammunition to fire ten thousand rounds each. Lord knows what other equipment they have at this base of theirs, or when and how they plan to strike."

"Have you tried trailing the trucks, sir?"

"Naturally. We concentrated on the Bishop Plant. We know the set-up there, of course. There's a manager named Brandon, in charge of the plant. When he first was promoted to the job, an investigation was made by the Bishop people. It didn't turn up a thing against him; his past was spotless. But now, when we made an investigation of our own, we found plenty. His name isn't Brandon at all. It's Krauswitz. Twenty years ago, he was a professor of chemistry at Hamburg. He came over here and changed his name, and was supplied with forged papers, including naturalization papers. He's running that plant, and he's diverting the Brownings. They've got a couple of hundred Japs working in the loading sheds, sleeping in secret cellars underneath. The loading sheds are separated from the plant proper, so that the workmen never have a chance to see what goes on there. They simply put half the stuff in the trains on the sidings, and at night they put the other half on trucks and drive away."

"It would seem simple enough to follow the trucks when they leave," Steve said.

"Not so simple, Steve. We dare not let them suspect that we're on to the game, because they'll just move their base, or disperse and form somewhere else. We have to follow them discreetly. But when our men do that, the trucks turn out to be going on perfectly harmless missions. They drive to a dock or a warehouse and unload, with their papers in perfect order. Every one of their trucks is tailed by another car, which signals to them if they're followed. You see, every defense plant expects a certain amount of surveillance, so they don't consider it strange that some of their trucks are tailed. But if we tried tailing every one of the trucks leaving the plant, they'd immediately understand that we had concrete suspicions."

"I see," said Stephen Klaw. He drew a deep lungful of cigarette smoke, exhaled it, and met his Chief's eyes. "Kerrigan and Murdoch and I will go right to work on it, sir," he said.

THE CHIEF smiled wearily. "I knew you'd volunteer. We've lost eight men who tried working their way into the plant. But I've got to ask you to do it. It's imperative that we locate that secret base."

He went to the door with Steve. "All the Facilities of the F.B.I.—and of the Army—are at your disposal. There is only one piece of information I can give you that may be helpful: each of these plants, including the Bishop plant, communicates by short-wave radio with this secret base. We've intercepted and decoded several messages, so that we know they get in touch with someone at the base whenever an emergency arises. *But the Base itself never sends on shortwave.*"

"They're too cagey for that," said Steve. "They know you could locate them with directional finders. And they also know that any one of these plants may be caught any time."

The Chief smiled wryly. "But they also know that we wouldn't raid a plant, even with all the evidence in the world. They know we'd do just what we're doing now—lie low and hope for a break that might lead us to the Base."

Stephen Klaw suddenly smiled. "I have an idea, sir. Could

you assign us one of those new Douglas Bombers, with an army pilot"

"I'll see that it's done at once!"

"And clear the skies around the Bishop Plant tonight, so we won't run into any Army Interceptors. Johnny and I will be wearing German uniforms, and we don't want to be shot by our own boys."

"All right, Steve. But what's your plan?"

"With your permission, sir, we'll see if we can't feed the enemy some taffy. Dan Murdoch will go into the Bishop Plant, and raise unholy hell. Then Johnny and I will appear—"

"Masquerading as officers from their Base"

"Right!"

"It's too dangerous, Steve. This Krauswitz will probably know all the Base officers—"

"I'm counting on the fact that he's a well-disciplined man, who will not dare to question authority. It's worth the chance."

The Chief nodded. "All right," he said. "Good luck!"

CHAPTER 2
TWO-MAN RIOT SQUAD

A LIGHT flickered, two thousand feet below; an ultra-violet light, visible only through a special glass. It flicked five times in quick succession, then once, then five times again.

Stephen Klaw, lying flat on his stomach at the bombardier's sight in the belly of the bomber, spotted it at once; the bombsight had been equipped with the special glass which made it possible to see the short light-waves.

He called back to Kerrigan, who was in the after-gun compartment. "That's it, Johnny!"

Lieutenant Cooper, in the pilot's seat, asked, "Shall I drop a flare, Steve?" he asked.

"Hell, no!" Klaw exclaimed. "That would, give the show away. Pull up to about five thousand, and circle around slowly."

Lieutenant Cooper sent the Douglas into a steep climb, and levelled off at five thousand. Kerrigan and Klaw both made their way forward, and Klaw slipped into the co-pilot's seat. He put the earphones on his head.

"Calling Murdoch," he said into the speaker, "calling Murdoch. Klaw standing by at five thousand. Come on in, Dan."

He flipped the hand switch over, and a moment later he caught Murdoch's voice. "Murdoch calling. I hear your motor, Steve. You're directly overhead. I'm signalling from the Bishop Plant. I'm on the roof of Assembly Building Number Three. It's the stuff, all right. There's an open field a half mile due east. You can come down there. When you get to the main gate, give me two shorts and two longs on your whistle, and I'll start the show. Signing off… Acknowledge!"

"Got you, Dan," said Stephen Klaw. "We'll be with you in ten minutes. Hang on, Mope!"

He removed the earphones. His eyes met those of Johnny Kerrigan in a significant glance. "Let's go, Johnny!"

They both had parachutes strapped and ready on their backs. Kerrigan had a Krupp submachine gun strapped on in addition, and Steve Klaw was equipped with a belt of grenades. They both wore the coveralls and helmet of parachute troops, but everything about them, including their weapons, was of foreign manufacture. To look at them, anyone would have sworn that they were members of an Axis invasion force.

Klaw raised his hand in signal, and Lieutenant Cooper pressed a button. Immediately, a double door in the floor of the cabin slid open.

Kerrigan and Klaw stood at the edge of the opening, while the plane circled and steadied, and Lieutenant Cooper studied his instruments.

Suddenly the lieutenant called out, "Now! And don't you fellows forget to count ten!"

Steve waved to him, and jumped. Johnny Kerrigan followed, almost on his heels. The two figures went spinning down through the void, while the plane roared away into the night.

Stephen Klaw counted to ten and pulled his rip-cord, tensed his muscles to take the shock of the opening bag. A second later, Johnny Kerrigan did the same, and then they were both riding easily in the sky.

WORKING IN unison, they maneuvered their chutes so as to land in the field Murdoch had mentioned. There was a slight east wind, but they skillfully swung the chutes around when they hit the ground, to avoid being dragged by them. A moment later they were unbuckling themselves out of the unwieldy harness, and rolling up the chutes.

"That was a nice ride, Shrimp," Johnny Kerrigan said. "You think we were spotted coming down?"

"I hope so," said Steve. "It'll simplify things when we get to the gate."

They cut across the field to the road.

"Let's ditch our chutes in the ditch," said Johnny. "We can pick them up later."

They put the folded gear in the ditch alongside the road. Then they both set off swiftly toward the Bishop Plant, whose lights they could see clearly, a half mile away. They did not remove their flying coveralls,

but they zipped the tops half way down, exposing the shiny Iron Crosses, Second Class, which each of them wore on his tunic.

"Veil, veil!" Johnny Kerrigan grinned. "Ve are now two officers of the Reich Secret Expeditionary Army in America. Vat iss your name, my goot friendt?"

Stephen Klaw puffed out his chest, thrust his chin out. "I am *Oberleutnant* Carl Cassel, at your service, *Excellentz!*" he said in perfect German.

Johnny Kerrigan's eyes twinkled. "And I," he replied in just as pure German, "am *Kapitan* Walther von Schön." He added in English, "And don't forget to address me with the deference due my rank, chum!"

Steve made the sound of the raspberry, and then raised his hand and said, *"Heil Shicklgruber!"*

"Don't make a mistake and say that when we're talking to our friends!"

"If you ask me," said Steve, "if I were Hitler, I'd have changed my name to Cohen, long ago. Some day, he's going to wish his name was Cohen, so he could live in obscurity in some nice quiet concentration camp."

"Not he," said Johnny. "His kind has always got to be the center of the stage. He'll want to go out in a blaze of glory. He'll probably douse himself with synthetic gasoline, and set fire to himself on the steps of that Munich beer garden."

"Nice thought," Steve commented. "But take it easy now. Here's the main gate of the Bishop plant. Watch your step, or *we'll* go out in a blaze of glory!"

They could see at a glance that there was a lot of excitement inside the gates of the plant. A dozen arc-lights just inside the grounds threw a ghastly glare upon the milling crowd of fifteen or twenty guards in the yard. Several revolvers were in evidence, and a couple of them were taking pop shots at the roof of one of the buildings.

Steve and Johnny began to run toward the gate. A large signboard at the side of the road proclaimed that this was the BISHOP WHEEL AND AXLE CORPORATION.

Underneath the name, someone had pasted a strip sheet with the following lettering in red:

NOW ENGAGED IN DEFENSE WORK
ALL UNAUTHORIZED PERSONS FORBIDDEN
TO ENTER

The shooting within the yard continued, but there were no answering shots from the roof of the building which was the target. That building had a huge number 3 painted in red alongside the doorway.

"That's the building Dan is on!" Steve exclaimed, as they ran. "He isn't returning their fire. Either he's lying low, or they got him with a lucky shot!"

"If they got him," Johnny Kerrigan panted grimly, "I'll take 'em apart two by two, and put them together again—cockeyed!" **THEY CAME** racing up to the gate, and Johnny took hold of it and shook it. He shouted in a thick voice which he made quite guttural, "Open! Open the gate quickly!"

A man detached himself from a small group, and came over and put his face close to the bars. He was a small man, with

87

narrow eyes, and very dark hair. He looked at them keenly, studying their clothing, observing the unmistakable fact that the guns in their holsters were German Lügers. Then he noted the Iron Crosses on their tunics.

"Ah!" he said in German, "you have then come from Base A!"

"Open up, you fool!" Johnny Kerrigan snapped curtly in German. "Do you dare to waste time with your babble when there is an emergency?"

"I am sorry, *Excellenz,*" the man said hastily.

He blew a whistle, and motioned imperiously to a guard, who hurried over and unlocked the gate. Stephen and Johnny stepped swiftly inside, and the gate was locked again after them.

The men who had been sniping at the roof of Building Number Three ceased firing when they saw the two new arrivals. The thin man with the narrow eyes bowed subserviently to Johnny and Steve.

"I am *Doktor* Krauswitz," he said in German, "the manager of this plant. I assure your Excellencies that I am entirely at your service."

"*Kapitan* von Schön." Johnny bowed from the hips, in elegant military style. Then he motioned toward Steve. "My adjutant, *Oberleutnant* Cassel."

"Indeed, yes," *Doktor* Krauswitz said eagerly. "It seems that a number of men managed to gain entrance to the plant. There must be at least ten of them, all well-armed."

Johnny Kerrigan barely suppressed the laughter within him. He glanced at Steve Klaw, and saw that he, too, was having difficulty keeping a straight face. For they both knew that Dan Murdoch was the only man making the trouble.

Krauswitz said, "We have already killed two or three of them, yet they continue to shoot from different portions of the roof, all at the same time. *There!*" He raised a finger and pointed.

Three shadowy figures were visible on the roof, peering over the coping at one corner. At the other corner, there were four more shadowy figures. Six of the shadowy figures fired simultaneously, while the seventh stood up and nonchalantly tossed a grenade down into the yard. Then all seven figures ducked back out of sight.

The grenade exploded in the corner of the yard farthest from the spot where *Herr Kapitan* von Schön and *Oberleutnant* Cassel were standing. It tore a crater in the concrete, and the detonation shook the whole yard. But nobody was injured, because every man had sprinted for cover. The only ones who remained standing on their own feet without cover were the pseudo captain and the pseudo lieutenant. Even *Doktor* Krauswitz had ducked, throwing himself flat on the ground, in the shelter of the guard's shanty close to the gate.

Johnny and Steve grinned at each other. Murdoch had been careful to keep that grenade as far from them as possible.

Krauswitz dusted himself off, and looked shamefacedly at Johnny. "Perhaps," he ventured, "perhaps we should take shelter? One can never tell when those madmen will stand up again—"

"We will remain here," Johnny said coldly. One who fears to lose his life is of no use to the *Fuehrer!*"

"Of course, of course!" Krauswitz said.

"And now, permit me to tell you, *Herr Doktor*, that you are a fool!"

"I do not understand, *Excellenz*—"

"You do not need to understand. I shall now demonstrate to you how a matter like this should be handled. *Oberleutnant* Cassel and I will capture or kill these madmen for you!"

"But—but it is too dangerous, *Herr Kapitan*. There is no access to the roof, except by a narrow skylight, and they would shoot you down like dogs as you showed your heads—"

"We do not need your advice!" Johnny said haughtily. He motioned to Steve.

Steve gave him a snappy salute. They both drew their heavy Lügers, and moved across the yard toward Building Number Three. The guards watched them goggle-eyed.

Johnny and Steve stopped within twenty feet of the building, and Johnny motioned to Steve, who cupped his hands and called up to the roof, in German, "You men, up there! We call upon you to surrender. Show yourselves, with your hands in the air!"

From the roof there came a scattered volley, which went high over everybody's heads. But the guards all scampered for cover.

Johnny and Steve remained alone in the yard. Steve winked at Johnny, cupped his hands again, and called out, this time in English: "Since you do not surrender, we shall come and get you!"

The only answer from the room was a derisive shout.

Johnny and Steve started toward the building.

Doktor Krauswitz came running over to them. "Please be careful, Excellencies. The building is vacant, we do not use this particular building on the night shift. It may be that some of those Yankee devils will ambush you inside the building—"

"Silence!" Johnny thundered. "Do you dare to offer advice to a German Captain?"

"No, no," poor Krauswitz murmured. "Forgive me…"

CHAPTER 3
MADAME SYLVAIN

T HEY LEFT him standing there, and hurried in the building. The great, vast assembly shop was deserted, and their footsteps echoed and re-echoed as they went up the iron stairs to the narrow balcony which circled underneath the roof. They found the ladder which led up to the skylight, and Steve went first, with Johnny close behind him. They looked down, and saw that a small collection of guards had come in to watch them. The guards were evidently quite sure that the captain and the lieutenant would meet their death up at the skylight.

Steve and Johnny made a great show of climbing up cautiously, and when Steve got to the top rung he raised his Lüger, waited a moment dramatically, then fired four times into the glass. He covered his face with his arm to protect it against the falling glass, then he knocked out the rest of it with the barrel of his gun. He pushed his head up through the opening, and saw Dan Murdoch standing close to the skylight.

"Hi, Mope," he said.

"Hi, Shrimp," Dan Murdoch said, grinning.

They both raised their guns and fired three shots rapidly into the air. Then Steve climbed up swiftly through the frame of the skylight, giving the impression to those on the floor far below that he was going over the top.

Johnny Kerrigan followed him, and in a moment the three of them were in a huddle on the roof. They kept shooting, making a continuous barrage of noise, and Steve Klaw even took out one of his grenades and threw it to the far end of the roof, where it detonated with frightful noise, blowing away part of the parapet.

"Nice going, guys," said Murdoch, as they kept up the barrage into the air. "I see you've got them eating out of your hand."

"Listen, Dan," Steve Klaw demanded. "How the devil did you make them believe there were ten of you?"

Murdoch chuckled, and pointed to a row of sand sacks along the parapet. He had nine or ten of them propped upright against the parapet, with long ropes tied to each, and he had the ends of those ropes all bunched in one hand. In the other hand he had the ends of another series of ropes, the other ends of which were tied to the triggers of rifles, which were, in turn, lashed to the dummies.

"It's all a matter of sandbags and psychology," he said. "I found the bags and the rope up here, all ready for an air raid. I rigged them up like this, and every time I want to give them a blitz, I go around and stand the dummies up, pull the strings, and let the shots fall where they may."

"All right," said Steve. "Let's be going. The idea now is to see if we can kid these birds into sending us back to Base A with a chauffeur."

"Well," said Murdoch, "we can only try. Strange things have

been known to happen." He raised his gun and fired a few more shots.

"Think that'll give them enough excitement?" Murdoch asked.

"I guess that's enough," Johnny said. He grinned at Dan. "You are now our prisoner, *Herr* Murdoch. Kindly descend—and remember, no tricks!"

MURDOCH GAVE them his gun, and they went over to the skylight. Peering down, they saw a small sea of faces turned upward from the floor below.

"I better put on a good act," Murdoch said, and raised his hands in the air.

The three of them descended the ladder, Klaw first, then Murdoch, then Kerrigan.

Doktor Krauswitz was waiting for them, rubbing his hands, while the guards stood a few feet away, their mouths hanging open.

"Wonderful, Excellency!" exclaimed Krauswitz. "You have wiped them out, and even managed to capture one of their number! It was marvelous! We saw how you went fearlessly upon the roof. Two against ten—"

"You fool!" said Kerrigan. "There was only one man. He tricked you. He has made fools of all of you!"

It took Krauswitz and the others some time to convince themselves that there had been but one man. The *Doktor* wrung his hands in shame. His eyes blazed hatred at Murdoch.

"You have made of me a laughingstock, you *verdammter*

93

schwein!" He snatched his revolver out of its holster, and rushed at Murdoch.

Klaw deftly tripped him. "Your pardon, *Herr Doktor*. My foot must have got in your way." He lifted him by the collar and poked a fist close to his nose. "Next time, this will get in your way, my stupid friend!"

Krauswitz was trembling. His nose was scraped where it had rubbed against the concrete. Kerrigan looked at him severely. "You fool, do you wish to kill our prisoner before we can question him?"

"I am sorry, Excellency—"

"Take us to the sheds."

Krauswitz led the way across the grounds toward the railroad siding. This portion of the grounds was screened from the rest of the buildings by a high wall.

They passed through a door in the wall, and saw a dozen trucks backed up to the loading platform, with small, wiry Japanese busily loading crates into them.

Steve whispered to Kerrigan, "Those crates contain Browning automatic rifles! Boy, they're figuring on using our own guns against us!"

"Let's splash them all over the countryside!" Kerrigan growled. "We've got enough grenades—"

"Nix," said Steve. "Our job is to discover the location of Base A. We can take care of this place, later."

"All right," Johnny grumbled.

They marched Murdoch, with his hands still in the air, over to the loading platform.

"And now," said Kerrigan, frowning sternly at Krauswitz, "we will take our prisoner to Base A. Kindly select a truck which is ready to leave, and instruct the driver to make room for us."

Kerrigan, Murdoch and Klaw waited tensely to see if the stunt would work. It seemed almost too simple and easy to be true. Krauswitz was eating out of their hand.

"It happens, Excellency," he said, "that we have a young woman here, waiting also for transportation to Base A."

"A young woman?" Johnny asked.

"It is no doubt someone you know, Excellency. She is a very valuable agent—Madame Sylvain. She operates now under the name of Leonora Westlake, in the best of American society!"

"Westlake!" exclaimed Steve. He exchanged a swift glance with Kerrigan. The name was familiar to them, of course, for they had seen it in the society columns. She was foreign born, but she had married Tony Westlake, the polo player, who had been killed in an accident several years ago. Since then she had, as Krauswitz said, mixed in the best social circles. But no finger of suspicion had ever pointed to her.

MURDOCH, WHO had been permitted by his "captors" to lower his hands, moved over close to Steve, and whispered, "That Westlake dame is bad news for us, Steve. She knows us. Remember, she was at the State Department Ball last year. She was introduced to us!"

Krauswitz was hurrying toward a small shack near the loading platform. "I will get her," he called back. "She will be glad for such distinguished company!"

"Ouch," said Steve Klaw. "This hurts. Just when we were sailing along okay—"

"I'll call him back," Johnny whispered.

"Too late," said Murdoch. "She's seen us. I just saw her face in the window, and she stepped back when she saw me looking. She's recognized us, chums."

Krauswitz was already stepping into the shack.

"Looks like we don't get to Base A," said Steve.

"Here goes nothing!" said Johnny Kerrigan. He unslung the machine gun from his back, and handed it to Murdoch. "Here, prisoner. Go to work!"

Murdoch grinned. "It was nice while it lasted!"

The woman had lost no time in telling Krauswitz the true identity of his two important visitors and the prisoner. For almost at once, his whistle began to blow, apparently in the signal used for an alarm, and the guards came running into the shed. At the same time, the Japanese workmen at the loading platform dropped their work and produced weapons from under their blouses.

Krauswitz came running out of the shack and pointed at Kerrigan, Murdoch and Klaw.

"*Verdammte* Yankees!" he screamed. "Kill them! Kill!"

"Sure," said Johnny Kerrigan. "Kill is right!" And he snapped a shot at Krauswitz.

The doctor went down just as the attack began. The guards came in from one side, the Japanese from the other. The guards came in firing haphazardly, but the Japanese suddenly lined up at the sharp blast of a whistle, in military formation, with a small, wiry Jap at their head. The man uttered swift commands, and the line moved forward toward the three Americans, firing as they came.

Dan Murdoch was already down on one knee, making the machine gun sing, and the first line of Jap attackers went down. Johnny Kerrigan was facing in the other direction, standing spraddle-legged, with his own gun in one hand, and Klaw's gun in the other, sending blast after blast into the guards.

Stephen Klaw had given Kerrigan his gun, because he needed both hands. He was pulling the pin from his first grenade when the Japanese line reformed. He threw it swiftly, putting plenty of zip into the pitch, and a mushroom-like explosion enveloped the Japanese.

Klaw sent two more pineapples into their ranks, and that broke them for the moment. He heard Murdoch's machine gun chattering in the other direction, saw that Dan was taking care of the remainder of the guards. But he also saw blood on Murdoch's chest....

Kerrigan noticed it at the same time, and seized hold of him, just as Murdoch dropped the machine gun.

For a moment there was a clear path through the broken ranks of the Japs, and Steve yelled, "This way!" He took his gun back from Kerrigan, and they moved forward, shooting as they went.

The leader of the Japs must have been stunned or grazed by a bullet. He had fallen, momentarily, right in the path of the advancing G-men, with a gun in his hand.

Stephen Klaw had emptied his automatic, and Johnny Kerrigan was supporting Murdoch with one hand, and firing at the Japs with the other.

Klaw said, "Nuts!" and leaped at the Jap. He caught him around the neck, and the two of them went down. The wiry little fellow was powerful, and tricky. He smashed back with both elbows at Steve's solar plexus, but Steve had anticipated that, and he twisted around, arcing his body with the blows. He bent and swung one arm underneath the Jap's leg, lifted him high in the air, and hurled him at the nearest of the Japs, who had come charging in to rescue their leader.

Johnny swung his free hand around, and sent the last remaining shots into that group, and for the moment they were free of attack. They sprinted toward the nearest of the trucks at the loading platform, and Steve hurled one more grenade, which gave them time to climb in.

Murdoch said, "I'm all right, Steve. Give me a couple of pineapples!"

Steve handed him two of them, and as Kerrigan slipped behind the wheel, they both hurled their eggs. The thunderous detonations mingled with the echoes of the other explosions.

Kerrigan sent the truck hurtling down the road, across the railroad siding and out of the plant.

There was another truck, about a quarter of a mile ahead of them, and Kerrigan pointed it out to Steve.

"That's the Westlake dame—alias Madame Sylvain. She scrammed the minute the fight started. Let's catch her—"

"Nix!" said Steve. "Slow up, Johnny. Let her go."

Kerrigan gave him a queer look. Murdoch, who was wiping the blood from a wound in his side, grinned.

"The Shrimp is right, Johnny. Let her go. She's more valuable to us outside of jail. Krauswitz had no time to tell her that he had mentioned her name to us. For all she knows, we're still ignorant of her identity. We've flopped here, but we can try again. We'll contact her, somehow, and maybe she'll lead us to Base A, next time!"

CHAPTER 4
THE KISS OF DEATH

STEPHEN KLAW leaned back drunkenly in the luxurious limousine, and gazed admiringly at the dark, beautiful woman beside him.

"Gawjeous," he said. "Simply gawjeous!"

The woman smiled. She wore an ermine cape over a daring red evening gown. Her black hair was piled high on her head, with a diamond-studded pin thrust through the coils. That pin was long enough, and strong enough, to be used as a dagger. But, of course, such a thought would not occur to a man like Stephen Klaw, steeped in drunken admiration.

She laughed a tinkling little laugh, and put one cool hand on his. "Who is gorgeous?" she asked.

Klaw grinned fatuously. "You are, my dear Leonora. You know you are. Everybody must tell you that. I'm a lucky guy to be invited to this party with you."

He hiccupped violently. Then he said, "Excuse me." He leaned toward her, a suspicious look in his eye. "You sure you invited me jus' because you like me?"

"Of course!" she said. "Why else should I invite you? The Gilpins told me over the phone to bring along someone I liked. And we were having such a good time at the night club, that I didn't have to look any further."

"Yeah," said Stephen Klaw, wiggling a finger at her. "I'm not so sure. Maybe you're a female spy."

She laughed—a forced laugh. "You're so funny, Steve!"

"You're sure you didn't invite me on account of these plans that I told you about?"

"Look here, Stephen Klaw," she said angrily. "If you're going to insult me, we can call this off. I'll tell the chauffeur to turn around and drop you off somewhere. It's too bad you can't forget you're a G-man for a few hours—"

"Can't ever forget," Steve mumbled, thickly. "Always on my mind. Shouldn't be here with you now. Should be getting some sleep. Got to get to work on these plans tomorrow." He tapped his torso with one hand. "Got the plans in an oilskin pouch right here, next to my liver. Can't afford to take chances." Then he suddenly grinned at her. "But you're all right, Leonora. You're no spy, are you? You wouldn't try to get 'em away from me, would you?"

"What do *you* think?" she asked softly.

"Hah!" said Steve. "Can't ever tell about a woman. Mata Hari was beautiful, too. Remember her?"

Yes," said Leonora. There was a strange look in her eyes. "Yes, I remember her. They said she was caught because of a moment's weakness." She changed the subject swiftly. "But you look so young to be entrusted with valuable plans."

"Yeah," said Steve. "That's what they all tell me. But *this* is what counts!"

His hand hadn't seemed to move, yet suddenly there was a small, snub-nosed automatic in it. He grinned at the quick flicker of fear in her face, and slipped the weapon back under the jacket of his tuxedo.

"Drunk or not," he said owlishly, "it'll take some tall hustling to get these plans off my body!"

"Let's not talk about that," Leonora said hastily. She shuddered. "I loathe the sight of guns."

"All right," said Steve. "What'll we talk about?"

"What of your two friends, Kerrigan and Murdoch?"

"Hah! So you know about them?"

"Of course I do. Who doesn't? Everybody has heard of the Suicide Squad. Where are Kerrigan and Murdoch now?"

Steve gave her that owlish look again. "A secret," he told her. "They both have copies of these plans. Tomorrow, we meet at a certain place, an' carry them out. When we finish, there'll be nine thousand Japs less to worry about!"

"Nine thousand Japs!" she exclaimed. "That's a small army. Where are they?"

"Right in this city!"

"I SEE!" whispered Leonora. "That means that a small Japanese army is ready to go into action, right at our backs!"

"Exactly!" said Klaw. "I shouldn't be telling you this, Leonora.

It's a military secret. You could get me court-martialed and shot if you let on that I told you."

"You can trust me!" she said with a smile.

"Sure, baby. Sure I can trust you. You're no Mata Hari. You're just the most beautiful woman in the world." He caressed her arm. "I'm a lucky guy to've met you tonight—"

But she brought him back to the subject. "Do you know where this army of Japs is hiding?"

"Uh-huh. Kerrigan, Murdoch and I found out yesterday. We reported, and got our orders—sealed orders—for tomorrow. Tomorrow we wipe 'em out!"

The limousine had slowed down, and was turning into the driveway of a suburban estate. The house at the top of the knoll, toward which they headed, was brilliantly lighted, and there were more than a dozen expensive cars parked around the semi-circle of the graveled space around the portico.

"Here we are," said Leonora. "Let's enjoy the evening. Let's forget all about your horrid plans for tomorrow."

Her cool fingertips touched his cheek, and she leaned toward him so that he caught the exquisite scent of the perfume of her hair. "Can't you forget you're a G-man, just for tonight?"

"Baby," Stephen Klaw grinned, "I've already forgotten it!"

He stumbled a little as he got out, and the chauffeur had to support him. But Klaw waved the man aside, and took Leonora's arm to help her out of the car. He jerked his head at the man, and winked. "He thinks I'm drunk. He's crazy."

Leonora gave him a queer glance. "I wonder," she said.

They went into the great house, and were announced by a tall and sallow-faced butler, who welcomed Leonora but gave Steve a supercilious stare.

"Good evening, Miss Westlake," he said. "It's good to see you again."

He led them into an enormous room, gayly lit, where people were standing around in small groups with drinks in their hands, engaged in animated conversation. In a corner, a girl was playing the piano; two or three couples were dancing.

The host, Andrew Gilpin, came forward to street Leonora.

"I'm glad you were able to make it, Leonora!" he exclaimed. He was a stout man, with a round, good-natured face and a pair of shrewd, twinkling eyes.

Leonora introduced him to Stephen Klaw, and he said, "Ah! I've heard of you, of course. You and your two partners have made history in the F.B.I. Too bad they aren't here, too."

Gilpin took them around and introduced them to half a dozen other people, and at once Steve was being monopolized by several beautiful girls.

He talked with them for a while and accepted a cocktail from the butler. He tossed the drink off at a gulp, put the glass back on the tray before the butler could move away.

Leonora had exchanged a few whispered words with Andrew Gilpin, and now she came over to the group, pushed through the girls who were crowded around Steve.

"You promised you'd dance with me first," she said.

"Sure!" Steve put his arm around her, and they moved out on the floor. His arm tightened around her waist.

"Baby," he said, "did I tell you you're gorgeous?"

103

Her body was soft and yielding against his; she smiled up at him. "Tell me more. I like to hear it—from you."

He maneuvered her over to the French doors, and out on the terrace. He did not release her, but pressed her closer. Her lips were close to his, and she did not resist when he kissed her. **THEY WERE** interrupted by a queer sound which emanated from the pitch blackness of the grounds outside. It sounded clear and sharp, unmistakably the hoot of an owl.

"To-whoo... to-whoo...."

Steve frowned. He took his arm from around her waist.

"Owls!" he said. "Have they got owls here?"

She shrugged. "I wouldn't know."

From somewhere else on the grounds, there came an answering cry: *"to-whee.... to-whoo...."*

"There's another," said Leonora.

Steve said, "Hah! A whole colony of them! I'm superstitious about owls." He was lighting a cigarette, having offered her one. And now, instead of throwing the match away, he held it up in two fingers, allowing it to burn down almost to the bottom before discarding it.

"Why did you do that?" Leonora asked sharply.

He grinned. "Scare the owls away. They don't like fire."

At that moment, Andrew Gilpin came out on the terrace.

"Ah, there you are, Leonora!" he exclaimed. "I was looking for you. Mrs. Gilpin is ill. Headache or something. I told her you were here, and she insists on saying hello to you. Will you come up? I'm sure Mr. Klaw will excuse you."

"Sure," said Steve. "Go ahead. I'll finish this cigarette."

He stood very still after they had left, facing the lighted room, his back to the grounds. He waited that way for perhaps two minutes before he heard the faint rustling behind him. Still he did not move.

The rustling continued, came closer, until it was audible directly beneath the terrace.

"*To-whoo....*"

Steve raised the cigarette to cover his mouth with his hand.

"Lay off that owl stuff, Johnny," he said. "You sound like a sick cat."

"Nuts to you, Shrimp," said the owl.

"Did you have any trouble following us?" Steve asked.

"Not a bit. Dan and I came in separate cars, to make sure we wouldn't lose you. But we both got here. Dan is out there now."

"Yeah. I heard him. He was the sick owl."

"Next time," Johnny Kerrigan said pettishly, "*you* can be the owl, and *I* will be the handsome come-on guy who has the good time. I saw you and the dame in that clinch."

"You don't think she'd fall for a carrot-top like you, do you?"

Kerrigan's chuckle sounded from the darkness. "She didn't fall for anything. That clinch was part of her job. Do you know what she did while you were kissing her?"

"Sure," said Steve. "She picked my pocket. She took my shiny little automatic. I showed it to her while we were in the car, so she'd make a play for it. I just wanted to be sure we were on the right track."

"They're going to try to kill you, Shrimp," Kerrigan warned. "They want those plans pretty badly."

"No doubt."

"You lucky dog!" Johnny said bitterly. "You always get the break."

"We tossed for it," Steve reminded him.

"Yes, I know. And I meant to look at that coin of yours. You always win. I'll swear that coin has two heads!"

"Better scram now, Johnny," said Steve. "I've got to do my stuff."

The rustling sound was renewed. "Here it comes, Shrimp. Catch!"

Steve Klaw swung around, and raised a hand. He deftly caught the object which Kerrigan had tossed to him from the darkness. It was a small, snub-nosed automatic, a twin of the one which Leonora had picked out of his pocket.

"See you in hell, Shrimp," called Kerrigan.

"Keep the fires burning," Klaw called back cheerfully.

CHAPTER 5
MURDER MASQUERADE

H E SLIPPED the automatic into the snug pocket on the inside of his jacket, waited a moment more, and then stepped inside. He threaded his way among the dancing couples, avoided a girl who wanted to dance with him, and made for the staircase.

The sallow-faced butler seemed to appear from nowhere, at his elbow. "May I help you, sir? Was there anything you wanted?"

"Wha's your name?" Steve asked, making his voice a little thick.

"Bittrell, sir."

"Bittrell, eh? I've seen your face someplace. Are you a spy?"

The butler gave him a sickly smile. "I was about to go out on the terrace after you, sir. Mr. Gilpin asked if I would usher you to his library. He has some very special brandy he wants to have you sample."

"Brandy, eh?" said Steve. "Lead me to it."

"This way, sir."

Bittrell took him by the left arm, and guided him around the staircase and through a door which led into a short hallway. He opened a door at the left. "Right in here, sir."

Steve peered into the room. "This isn't the library—"

"But this is where we're going!" The butler's voice had suddenly become chill and hard. He retained his hold on Steve's left elbow, and with his left hand he brought out a small pistol. He pointed it at Steve. "Do you see what I mean?"

"Yes," Stephen Klaw said grimly. "I see what you mean!"

And he pulled the trigger of the snub-nosed automatic, which he had been holding under the jacket.

The shot didn't make much noise, muffled by the cloth of Steve's coat. The slug smashed into Bittrell's left arm, just above the elbow, and Bittrell uttered a hoarse cry. He dropped the pistol, letting go of Steve's elbow at the same time.

Klaw pushed him into the room, kicked the pistol inside, and followed him in. He closed the door behind them, and stood there for a moment, his eyes searching the place. It was a small sitting room. There was no one in there with them.

Bittrell had sunk into a chair. His face was ashen with pain, and he was holding his wounded arm. He glanced venomously at Klaw.

"Where did you get that automatic?" he demanded. "You were supposed to have been disarmed."

Steve laughed. "Is there supposed to be honor among spies?"

Bittrell's eyes widened. A spasm of pain twitched across his face, caused by his wounded arm, but he disregarded it. "The girl!" he spat out. "Leonora! She betrayed us! She told us she'd taken your gun!"

Steve shrugged. He didn't bother to disillusion the butler.

"I'm sorry to have to do this, Bittrell," he said. "But this is war. You don't deserve mercy; you're about as low as they come—a white man taking the pay of the yellow devils who are trying to destroy our country!"

He stepped in close, raising the automatic.

"You—you're not going to kill me!" Bittrell gasped, his face becoming the color of parchment.

"No," Steve said softly. "Not yet. I'll save you for the hangman! I'm just going to see that you're snug for a while."

He brought the barrel of the gun sharply down upon Bittrell's temple. The man collapsed. He toppled off the chair on to the floor, and lay still.

STEPHEN KLAW eyed him bleakly for a moment. Then he stooped and picked up the pistol which the spy had dropped. He raised his right trouser leg, and thrust the pistol in under his garter, where it rested snugly. He let his trouser leg drop over it. Then he slipped the automatic back into its pocket, and went to the door. He set the catch so that the door would lock when it was slammed, and stepped out into the corridor.

He could hear the piano playing in the ballroom, through the closed door down at the right end of the hall. But he went in the other direction, toward the left. He passed two other doors, but he did not open them. He went down to the end of the corridor, found a door there, pushed it open, and stepped through.

As he expected, he found a back staircase, which led to the upper part of the house. A man was standing guard at the foot of the stairs. He was dressed in servant's livery, but he was very evidently there for other purposes than those of service to wandering guests. He had a hard, square jaw, and powerful hands. There was the barely-concealed bulge of a gun in his hip pocket.

He said, "Were you looking for something, sir? These are the servants' quarters."

"It's all right," said Steve. "I'm going up to see Mr. Gilpin in the library. Bittrell suggested that I take the back staircase." He gave the man a significant look. "More privacy, you know."

"Sorry," said the man. "Orders are not to allow anyone up this stairway but the help." He moved over in such a way as to block Steve's progress.

"Well, that's too bad," said Stephen Klaw. He drove a left into the fellow's stomach, and met his advancing chin with a terrific right. The two blows sounded almost as one. That man must have weighed a hundred and eighty; and Stephen Klaw looked more like a college kid than like a tough scrapper. But that youthful look of his had been the undoing of more than one enemy. Behind that slim and boyish appearance, there was a hundred and sixty pounds of bone and muscle, trained to the last hairline of hardness. There was dynamite in that right, as the guard realized—too late. He was out, cold, before he hit the floor.

Steve sighed, rubbed his knuckles, and looked swiftly around. He saw a closet near the stairs, and hauled the unconscious man over to it. Working with speed, he used the man's own belt and garters and handkerchief to bind and gag him, then dumped him in the closet. He took the man's gun and kicked it under the stairs. Then, making sure that the closet door was closed, he went up.

The upper floor was quiet. But a hum of voices came from one room near the head of the stairs. Steve moved over to it, and stood very quietly. He could detect a man's voice and a woman's, then that of a third person, but he could not hear what they were saying.

HE GLANCED around, and saw that there was another door, only a few feet from this one. He went over and tried that, and found that it was unlocked. He turned the knob gently, and pushed it open a fraction of an inch. The room that this door opened into adjoined the library. It was in darkness. But he saw that it was connected with the library by an arched doorway. The sound of the voices came to him very plainly now. Andrew Gilpin was talking.

"I don't like it, Leonora," he was saying. "We're taking too much of a chance. If Bittrell falls down on the job—"

"How can Bittrell fall down on the job?" the third voice asked suavely. "We know that this Klaw is now disarmed. Here is the automatic, which Leonora took from him. He will be defenseless when Bittrell gets him into the room downstairs. It will only remain to hit him on the head and take the papers from him. Then we will have him taken out on the road, and run over by one of our cars. It will look like an unfortunate accident."

"Yes, I know," Gilpin interrupted. "But this damned Suicide Squad is too dangerous to fool around with. They're dynamite, I tell you!"

Stephen Klaw smiled at that. He moved into the darkened anteroom, closing the door carefully behind him. He heard Leonora Westlake's tinkling laugh.

"He's clever, that Klaw. And what a man! I'm sure he knew that I knew that he wasn't really drunk. And he as much as told me that he suspected me of being a spy. Yet he had the courage to come here."

"That's what I don't like about it," Gilpin grumbled. "It's not like the Suicide Squad to walk into an obvious trap—"

"That, my dear Gilpin," said the suave voice, "is where you are wrong. Believe me, I have studied this Suicide Squad carefully. And that is why I planned it this way. You see, it is not in the nature of those three men to avoid danger. The thing that brought this Klaw here was the scent of danger."

"But look here, Noltz," Gilpin exclaimed. "If he suspected a trap, what was to prevent him from having his friends—Kerrigan and Murdoch—follow him here?"

"Nothing at all, my dear Gilpin. In fact, one of them did

follow him. You see, I had Leonora's limousine followed by another car, at a discreet distance. In that way, we discovered that Leonora's limousine was being trailed by another car, driven by the dark-haired chap—Murdoch. He's somewhere on the grounds at this moment, but he shall be properly taken care of. You heard those owls hooting, didn't you? That was the signal Murdoch and Klaw exchanged, between themselves. Murdoch hooted from the grounds, and Klaw from the terrace. Murdoch was at once spotted by my men. They are no doubt watching him now. At the first move he makes, they will take care of him, never fear."

Standing in the dark, Stephen Klaw stiffened as he heard that smooth, suave voice of the man named Noltz, telling how Dan Murdoch would be taken care of. But almost at once, he heard Leonora Westlake speak tensely.

"Wait, *Herr* Noltz!" she exclaimed. "You said that Murdoch hooted like an owl, and that Klaw answered him?"

"Yes. Surely you heard the owl-hoots? Surely you understood—"

"I heard them!" Leonora said tensely. "I was on the terrace with Klaw when the owls hooted. There were two hoots!"

"Yes, of course. That's what I said."

"But," Leonora Westlake interrupted, "I told you, I was with Klaw on the terrace—*and he did not make any hooting sound!*"

For a long moment there was silence in the next room, while Stephen Klaw stood quiet. Then came the voice of *Herr* Noltz, no longer suave and smooth. *"Himmel!* There must have been *two* of them out on the grounds. I assumed there was only one, because only one car was observed following you."

"That fellow, Kerrigan, must be out there, too," Andrew Gilpin said. "They always work together, the three of them."

"I must warn the men!" Noltz exclaimed hurriedly. "Ludwig is on guard at the foot of the stairs. I will tell him—"

"I've already told him, my friend," said Stephen Klaw. He stepped out of the anteroom, his automatic significantly in evidence.

The three people in that room stared at him as if he had been a ghost.

STEVE SPARED only a glance at Leonora and Gilpin. He studied the man named Noltz. He was a thin man, about Steve's size and build, but with a hawk's nose, and a pair of predatory, merciless eyes. He stood tensely, his arms at his sides; but it was plain to be seen that he was ready to seize the first opportunity that presented itself.

Klaw grinned at him. "Relax, Noltz. You won't get any help from your pals." Then he turned to the woman. "Well, Leonora my dear, how goes the spy business tonight?"

She was frightened and desperate. She had thought that Klaw was safely dead or a prisoner by this time. Her lips twitched, but she did not speak.

It was Gilpin who answered.

"My dear Klaw, there must be some mistake. Surely you do not think that Leonora here is implicated in any spy undertaking."

Steve gave him a dry grin. "Skip it, Gilpin. I heard all I need."

113

It was in that moment, when Steve had apparently turned his head toward Gilpin, that Noltz chose to make his break. He leaped behind Leonora, threw one arm around her waist from behind, and drew a gun. He was shielded by her body from Steve's fire, and he didn't seem to care what happened to her.

"Stand still, you!" he ordered. "I am going to back out of the window. If you shoot, you will kill her."

Steve smiled. He spoke, apparently to someone behind Noltz's back. "Go easy, Dan. Don't kill him. We want him alive."

Noltz laughed sourly. "You cannot trick me that way!"

He stopped, gasping, as a revolver muzzle was thrust against his spine from behind. Dan Murdoch climbed in through the window.

"Just lay your gun down on the floor—easy!" Dan ordered.

For a second it seemed as if Noltz contemplated shooting Klaw anyway, and taking the slug in the spine as the price. Then he weakened.

"Don't shoot!" he whispered. Slowly and carefully, he bent down and put the gun on the floor.

Steve stepped in quickly, picked it up.

"Very nice co-ordination, Dan," he said. "Did you have trouble out there?"

"A little," said Murdoch. "Two guys were keeping their eyes on me. They had followed me all the way from town. They tried to jump me just now, but they didn't know Johnny was around. Too bad."

A moment later, Johnny Kerrigan appeared at the window, and climbed in. He grinned at the tableau.

114

"Hi, Owl!" he said to Steve.

"Owl yourself!" said Klaw. He gestured toward Noltz. "I think we have the big shot here, the guy who gives the orders all around. Maybe he can take us to Base A."

At the mention of Base A, Noltz started visibly, and glanced at Leonora. She gave him a viperish look in return.

"If I knew where the Base was," she said, "I'd tell them. You didn't care if Klaw shot me just now, did you? Well, I'll tell them everything I know. But—" she looked at Steve—"I swear I don't know where the Base is. You said you knew where it was."

"That was only a come-on," Steve told her. "I have no plans, for the simple reason that we don't know where the damned Base is located."

Noltz sneered. "And you will never know. You will never make me talk, be sure. "I—" he drew himself up to his full height—"am an officer of the German Army!"

"Indeed!" said Johnny Kerrigan. "So was I, yesterday. Shake, comrade!"

He grasped Noltz's hand behind him, twisted it around, and drew the helpless officer into the dark anteroom.

"Strip!" he ordered.

"WHAT'S THE idea, Johnny?" Steve called.

Kerrigan chuckled. "This guy is the Big Noise. He has a big car downstairs, with a chauffeur. I'm betting that the chauffeur is waiting to take him back to Base A."

Murdoch's eyes twinkled. "You're just about Noltz's size and height, Shrimp," he said.

Steve nodded suddenly. "Keep our guests company, Dan!"

115

He left Leonora and Gilpin under Murdoch's care, and hurried into the anteroom. In a couple of minutes he returned, attired in Noltz's blue suit, with Noltz's distinctive red-and-black necktie, and with Noltz's purple scarf wound around his neck.

In the meantime, Murdoch had effectively bound and gagged Gilpin, while Leonora Westlake looked on, making no effort to interfere. Kerrigan performed the same service for Noltz, in the anteroom.

As soon as they were through, Klaw went over to Leonora.

"A spy," he said slowly, "must always be prepared to pay the penalty if caught."

Her face was white, but she met his gaze.

"Yes," she whispered in a choked voice. "Do—do they hang spies in—in this country?"

"You know that as well as I do," Steve said.

She put a hand up to her throat. "I— I wouldn't enjoy hanging."

"Believe me," Steve said, "I'd spare you that if it were within my authority. But Kerrigan and Murdoch and I are only soldiers, doing our duty. It's our duty to turn you in."

She looked at him queerly for a moment. Then she said, "Even—even if I—helped you to reach Base A?"

"I can't promise you anything," Steve told her. "I can only tell you that I should have a strong distaste to seeing that pretty neck of yours stretched. If you helped us now, I'd have an even stronger distaste. It might be so strong that I'd have to do something about it."

She thought that over for a moment. "All right," she said at last. "I'll do whatever you say, and leave my life in your hands."

Steve nodded. Over his shoulder he said, "Get going, Mopes. I'll give you three minutes to get set in your cars. Keep your two-way radios going. Get in touch with the First Interceptor Command. Have them put bombers in the air. Call Army H.Q. and have them get the tanks rolling. *And for God's sake, don't lose us!*"

"Don't worry, Shrimp." Dan Murdoch laughed, as he climbed out the window after Kerrigan. "We'd hate to lose you. We're so used to you now!"

CHAPTER 6
"WALK AHEAD—TO HELL!"

FIVE MINUTES later, Stephen Klaw, with Leonora on his arm, crossed the grounds and approached a limousine near the outer rim of the parking circle in front of the house.

Klaw had the muffler wrapped well over the lower portion of his face, and he had Noltz's hat brim turned down as far as it would go over his eyes.

A man in chauffeur's uniform was sitting at the wheel, but when he saw the familiar figure of what he thought was Noltz, he jumped down and held the door open.

"There has been a little trouble out here, Colonel Noltz," he said. "Two G-men were skulking around. They got away."

Klaw motioned impatiently with his hand, and climbed in without answering. The chauffeur looked surprised, but Leonora

117

said to him, "The Colonel has been in a fight with one of those G-men. He was almost choked to death. His throat is sore. He wishes to go immediately to Base A. Hurry."

"Yes, Madame," said the chauffeur.

He closed the door, and got behind the wheel. In a moment they were rolling out of the driveway, on to the road.

Inside the car, Klaw and Leonora sat quietly, and Steve still kept his face covered. Once he glanced behind, but could not distinguish the shapes of any cars following them. He was not worried, however, for he knew that Kerrigan and Murdoch surely would have doused their headlights.

The chauffeur took the steep climb up the hill to the north and then swung west. Steve's pulse quickened. They were approaching the State Reservation. After ten minutes more driving along the outer edge of the Reservation, the chauffeur pulled to a stop alongside a thick copse at the side of the road.

He got out of the car and stood for a moment listening. Then he darted to the copse, pulled the boughs and twigs aside, revealing a sort of cave entrance.

"Hurry, please, Colonel and Lady," he said in German. "I think there is another car coming. Do not forget the password, my Colonel, or they will shoot."

Klaw and Leonora had already gotten out of the car. Klaw kept his face in the shadow as much as possible. He felt a cold shudder of disappointment as the man mentioned a password. He nudged Leonora, grunted, and motioned to the chauffeur.

The man looked puzzled. But Leonora was quick to grasp his

meaning. "Colonel Noltz cannot talk," she explained. "He wishes that you tell me the password, so that I can give it."

"Yes, Madame. The password tonight is *Yokohama*—"

He stopped abruptly as Klaw passed in front of him toward the mouth of the cave. "Wait! Colonel Noltz always uses perfume. You do not have perfume. You are not Colonel Noltz—"

"No," said Steve. "I never was!" And he hit him hard on the button.

The man went down like a log. Steve rubbed his knuckles. "*Yokohama!*" he murmured.

A moment later, two cars pulled up alongside the limousine. Kerrigan and Murdoch got out. Murdoch was carrying a portable sending and receiving set, such as he had used for contacting Steve from the Bishop Plant.

"It looks to me," he said, "as if Base A is located in the State Reservation!"

"Not a bad idea. They must have killed off the staff of rangers, and taken over their job. There's a thousand acres in that Reservation—enough to hide an army ten times nine thousand."

"Well," said Kerrigan, "what are we waiting for?"

Steve looked at Leonora. She stood still and tense, awaiting his word.

"You've done your part," he said. "You've helped us get this far." He glanced at Kerrigan and Murdoch. Murdoch was busy sending on the portable radio, but he nodded. Kerrigan nodded, too.

Steve turned back to her. "It's our, duty to turn you in, Leonora," he said. "If we let you go, we can be court-martialed."

He saw her shoulders sag. "I should have known!" she whispered. "I deserve it too. I've never kept my word to anyone. Why should I expect that you'd keep your word to me?"

Steve grinned. "Quite right, Leonora. So, in the name of the United States of America, I arrest you on the charge of espionage in time of war!"

"All right," she said. "I've lost. But please—shoot me. Don't let them hang me!

Steve was watching her closely. "Your usefulness as a spy is over, you know," he said casually. "Even if you escaped, you could never be a spy again. Your description and picture will be furnished to every American agent—"

"I'd never be a spy again!" she said passionately. "I have money now. I'd only want to be allowed to live somewhere, peaceably and forgotten. I'd—I'd even fight to keep this country the way it is."

Steve shook his head. "I'd like to believe you, Leonora. I'd like to give you a break. But it's against the rules. I can't let you go."

He turned his back on her, and winked to Kerrigan and Murdoch.

"The motor of that limousine is still running," he said casually over his shoulder. "And we three guys are abominable shots. If anyone should start driving rapidly away, I'm sure we'd never hit the car."

He heard her gasp behind him. "God bless you Kerrigan, Murdoch and Klaw!" she whispered.

Then, a moment later, they heard the clutch of the limousine grinding. The motor was accelerated, and the car sped away into the night.

Kerrigan breathed a sigh of relief. "I wouldn't have enjoyed seeing that dame hang!"

"Me, neither," said Klaw. "Let's get going!"

Murdoch got up from the ground, and thrust the radio sending set back into his car. "Okay, guys. I've been in touch with, the Army, the Navy, the Marines, and the Air Raid Wardens. Let's clear the way for them!"

KLAW WENT first into the cave, followed by Kerrigan and Murdoch. His flashlight showed a passage opening into the far end of the cave. They took it single file, and followed it for perhaps a hundred feet, when they came up into a small clearing.

"This must be inside the Reservation," Murdoch whispered.

Klaw, who was in the lead, checked them with an upraised hand. Fortunately, he had turned off his flashlight before stepping out into the clearing, for there was a small group of men standing there, all attired in full military uniform.

Five or six of them were Japanese officers, all of high rank, as was indicated by the collection of stars and bars on their tunics. There were two white men in the group, both attired in uniforms of the German Army. All were engaged in animated conversation. A little behind them, at a respectful distance, stood a squad of Japanese soldiers, with rifles unslung.

Kerrigan, Murdoch and Klaw remained in the shelter of the passageway, while that group of enemies talked in swift and excited voices, all in German.

One of the Japs was saying, "It is impossible for us to wait longer, Von Rudiger. Our contingent is ready to start. If it is to destroy the Grand Reservoir, it must leave now in order to return before daylight."

"But, General Yamanaka," the German protested, "it is important that we wait for the return of Colonel Noltz. We must have his report."

"Here he comes now," said General Yamanaka, as the sound of Kerrigan's safety catch on his automatic clicked in the night. "I hear him."

Kerrigan nudged Steve. "Go ahead, Shrimp. That's your cue!"

Klaw stepped out into the clearing, keeping his face muffled, and both hands in his pockets.

"Ah, Noltz!" said the German. "You are here at last! Why are you late? We have only been awaiting your report. Speak, man. What have you learned from Gilpin?"

"Nothing that will help you, General!" Steve said in English.

That group of officers acted as if a thunderbolt had hit them.

"It is not Noltz!" the German exclaimed.

The Jap General Yamanaka peered near-sightedly through the darkness at Steve. He raised a whistle which hung from his neck by a silver chain. But he did not yet put it to his lips.

"Who are you?" he demanded.

At the same time, the German backed inconspicuously away, and whispered something to a noncommissioned officer standing at the fringe of the group of general officers. That petty officer turned and issued low-voiced commands to the squad of guards, who immediately spread out, so as to flank the entrance from the tunnel.

But Steve apparently did not notice this furtive activity. He grinned at the Jap general and said casually, "The name is Stephen Klaw. I have a message for you from Gilpin."

"Ach!" said the German officer. "Klaw! It is one of the *verdammte* Suicide Squad! Believe him not, Yamanaka. He is poison— he and his two devil-companions. Order him taken—"

But Yamanaka, still with the whistle close to his lips, waved the German aside. His nearsighted eyes were still fixed upon Steve.

"This message you say that you have from Gilpin—what is it?"

Steve's hands were deep into his pockets now. He seemed to be lounging carelessly, but in reality he was as taut as the mainspring of a fully wound watch.

"Why, the message from Gilpin is that he'll see you in hell, Yamanaka!"

"Ah, so!" the Jap said sibilantly. "You are indeed a foolhardy man. You have come here alone perhaps? Or with your two friends? You think that alone you will break up this concentration of Imperial troops?"

"Don't worry," Steve said cheerfully. "We'll have company soon. The bombers are coming over any minute now. They'll blast hell out of you!"

He was talking against time now, for the bombers were overdue. Every moment that he managed to delay Yamanaka from giving decisive orders was so much to the good.

But the Jap general must have sensed his purpose. He glanced around and saw that the two squads of guards were disposed in such a position as to be able to rake Stephen Klaw with fire from two angles.

"You, my foolhardy friend," he said softly, "shall precede us to hell!"

He raised the whistle to his lips and blew a single shrill blast upon it.

THAT WAS the signal for the outburst of a devil's pandemonium. Both squads of soldiers raised rifles to their shoulders at the sharp singsong commands of their officers. At the same time, the whistle signal was repeated again and again beyond the screen of trees, where the main body of the Jap army was located. The entire striking force of the Japs was swinging into action.

Stephen Klaw brought his hands out of his pockets, with both automatics spitting fire. He was grinning a thin, death's-head grin as he directed both streams of hot lead into the center of that group of brass hats.

He paid no attention to the two squads of soldiers on his flanks. It was almost as if he were sublimely oblivious of their existence. To look at him there, standing there with both feet firmly planted, the guns barking and bucking in his fists, looking neither to the right nor the left, one would have thought that he was throwing his life away in a ridiculously useless manner; for there did not seem to be a chance that he could escape being mowed down by the cross-fire of those two flanking squads of yellow marksmen.

But the secret of it was that Stephen Klaw knew that he had two men at his back upon whom he could depend better than upon a whole army corps.

Kerrigan and Murdoch and Klaw had worked together for so long, and had faced odds of all kinds, that they operated with the smooth accuracy and perfect timing of precision machinery.

Almost at the sound of the first shot, Kerrigan and Murdoch stepped out from the tunnel behind him, and took up positions on either side of Stephen Klaw, their weapons thundering and roaring in a continuous, rhythmic threnody of thunder as they directed their fire at the two flanking groups.

The sudden barrage cut down those soldiers with deadly precision at the same time that Klaw's slugs smashed into the group of general officers. Then, in the moment of terrible confusion that followed, the three G-men began to move forward, shoulder to shoulder across the clearing, their guns still blasting.

Cries of excitement, confused orders in Japanese, and mingled yells of alarm arose from beyond the trees, where the main body of troops was swinging into emergency battle formation. But Kerrigan, Murdoch and Klaw moved forward, as if there had not been an army of nine thousand men facing them.

Someone began to fire at them with a machine gun, but the bursts were far too high and too wide. Still they kept moving forward, never stopping, never seeking cover.

They reached the spot in the clearing where the General Officers had stood. Above the rattle of gunfire, Klaw called out, "I can't hear the bombers, Mopes. It looks like we have to keep them entertained for a while longer."

Murdoch grinned. "Let's go!"

Just then, Klaw almost tripped over a prone figure writhing

at his feet. It was General Yamanaka. He had been shot in the stomach.

Steve stooped and picked him up. He was no longer a swaggering, blustering Imperial general, but just a little yellow man afraid to die. It was all well and good for the rank and file of the Japanese soldiers to be told that it was an honor and a glory to die for their Emperor. But these men of the General Staff knew that the Emperor was only a man just like themselves, and that he would never reward them in heaven.

Steve fell a pace behind Kerrigan and Murdoch as he helped Yamanaka forward. "You'll die if you don't get medical help quick, my general," he said.

Yamanaka had both hands at his stomach, trying to staunch the flow of blood. "A—doctor!" he gasped.

"Can you yell for one?" Steve demanded callously. "Can you yell loud?"

"I—will do anything you say—"

Steve picked up the whistle which hung from around Yamanaka's neck. It was a gold whistle, on a gold chain.

"How many blasts for retreat?"

"Two!" gasped the frightened Jap.

Steve raised the whistle to his lips and blew two shrill, high blasts upon it.

Almost at once, the two blasts were repeated by the petty officers ahead, and they could hear those two notes echoing in distant reverberations far back among the enemy lines.

The firing ceased completely, as if by magic.

Kerrigan and Murdoch turned around, grinning.

"Boy," said Kerrigan, "the whistle is mightier than the gun! I'd never have believed it!"

It was at that moment that the first formations of bombers came flying over the Reservation. It was a grand sight to see, as they swept across, dropping their flares, to be followed by a second wave, with bomb racks full.

But it was not necessary to drop a single bomb. Those Japs in Malaya and in Sumatra, where they outnumbered their enemies and had the weight of armament in their favor, rode high, wide and handsome. But here, in the heart of an alien country, seeing those mighty bombers overhead, and knowing they could not expect the support of anyone, they were small and frightened, just like their general. They stood there, with their hands held high in the air, shouting their surrender.

"Oh, hell!" said Johnny Kerrigan. "And I was looking for a scrap! These guys can't fight! Wait'll we get enough planes over there—"we'll be eating Japs for breakfast every morning!"

"Nah!" said Murdoch. "You can't eat Japs. They'd give you acid stomach. Me for a good, juicy steak all the time! What say?"

"Amen," said Stephen Klaw. "Let's go back to Gilpin's party. I bet there's a lot of eats left, over there. They must have lost their appetites completely by now!"

SO SORRY, MR. HIROHITO!

CHAPTER 1
RECEPTION!

STEPHEN KLAW arrived in the city of Valparaiso at four o'clock in the afternoon. He went directly to the Hotel Republica. When he signed his name in the register, the clerk said, "Ah! Señor Klaw!" and signalled to a group of newspaper men in the lobby. In a moment Klaw was surrounded by the members of the Latin press.

A tall Chilean reporter with a waxed moustache and a pair of twinkling eyes introduced himself first. "I am Miguel Santos, of the newspaper, *El Nación*, Señor Klaw. Welcome to Chile. We are all interested in your so famous F.B.I. And you, one of the most famous of its agents—"

"I'm not in the F.B.I.," Klaw said. "I resigned. I'm just down here as a private citizen."

Miguel Santos laughed. "Nevertheless, Señor Klaw, you have brought your gun, no?"

"Yes." Steve's eyes were suddenly twin pools of gray ice. "Yes, I've brought my gun."

Among the group of reporters were two Germans, a Jap, and an Italian. One of the Germans said sneeringly, "And for what purpose do you bring a gun to a neutral country like this, *Herr* Klaw?"

Steve turned his cold gaze on the man. "Scram!" he snapped. "And you, and you!" He looked from one to the other of the Axis reporters. "I don't give interviews to rats!"

Chile was indeed a neutral country. Its government, contrary to the instincts and feelings of the great majority of the population, had not yet seen fit to join the United Nations in the war against the Axis. So here, right in the western hemisphere, was a city where the enemies of the United States could carry on with impunity their sabotage and espionage. Americans and Englishmen in Valparaiso had to watch out constantly for a knife in the back.

The German reporter was a big, heavy-set man, with close-cropped hair and a square jaw. He took a step forward, towering over Stephen Klaw's slim, wiry figure.

"You American pig!" he growled. "You dare to insult me, Otto Betz! You must learn that here in Chile, a German is respected. I shall teach you some respect!"

He swung a huge, ham-like hand, endeavoring to slap Klaw's face.

Stephen Klaw's appearance was highly deceptive—as many a boastful killer had learned in the past, to his sorrow. Klaw was so slim and wiry that he looked hardly more than a kid just out of college. But in all the ranks of the Federal Bureau of Investigation there were only two men who, were as dangerous as he, his partners, Johnny Kerrigan and Dan Murdoch.

Herr Otto Betz, German newspaperman and holder of

the Iron Cross, had his lesson coming. His big paw never reached its mark. Stephen Klaw did not duck the blow, nor did he attempt to fend it off. His theory was that a good offensive is always the best defense. He stepped in close to *Herr* Betz. The German's arm fanned empty air behind Steve's neck, and at the same time, Steve drove a wicked right into the

German's paunch. His fist sank in, almost up to the wrist. Betz's breath expelled in a terrific, anguished gust.

Steve smiled and stepped away, his back to the counter. The other German and the Jap had been stepping in to help their associate, but when Steve faced them, they both stopped short.

Betz was doubled over with agony. His partner glared at Steve, but did not offer to attack. The Jap, however, clutched stealthily under his coat, and when his hand emerged, it held a knife.

Stephen Klaw had his left hand in his coat pocket. He brought it out, gripping a thirty-two calibre automatic. In the sudden silence in the lobby, the *snick* of the safety catch was loud and sharp.

He pointed the gun at the Jap with the knife. "So sorry to disturb your honorable intentions, Hirohaha," Klaw said with mock apology.

The Jap's eyes were bright and shiny behind his thick-lensed glasses. He stood immovable for a moment, then slowly began to push the knife back into its hidden sheath under his coat.

"Meestar Klaw," he said, "you are vairy reckless man. You not live long here in Valparaiso."

"Get out," said Steve.

THE JAP and the German helped Otto Betz out of the hotel lobby into the street, and the lone Italian newspaper man who had been with them faded away as inconspicuously as possible.

Miguel Santos and two or three other Latin reporters were all who remained. Santos was rubbing his hands. "Next to the war, Señor Klaw, you will be the biggest news in Valparaiso. You are what the North Americans call 'hot copy!'"

Steve grinned. "Fine city you've got here, Santos. But too many rats in it!"

"Tell us please," begged Santos. "Tell us of your mission in

Valparaiso. Is it true that you have come here to seek out and kill a—shall we say—*a certain person?*"

Steve's eyes flickered. "My dear Santos! How can you say such a thing? After all, I'm only a visitor here to your beautiful country. Would it be right for me to come with violent intentions?"

"It is common gossip, Señor," broke in another of the reporters, "that the person you have come to seek and kill is Gaston Zambetta!"

Steve shook his head. "Why should I make war on Gaston Zambetta?"

"It is said, Señor, that Zambetta did much sabotage in the States, and that he escaped upon the declaration of war, after killing an agent of your Federal Bureau of Investigation. It is said that no one has ever—what-you-call—'gotten away,' with the killing of a Federal Agent, and that you have come to track Zambetta down and avenge that deed."

Steve shrugged, smiling. "That would be a violation of your neutrality. After all, Zambetta enjoys the privilege of any other visitor to your country."

"Señor," said a third reporter, "what you tell us may be considered confidential. Believe me, we of the press are on your side. It is with our best wishes that you come with this challenge for Zambetta. But let us give you some advice. Gaston Zambetta is very powerful in Valparaiso. Here, the Axis has many killers at its command, and you are but one. Even if your friends, Murdoch and Kerrigan, should join you, it will be but three against a multitude—"

"Three has been our lucky number," Steve interrupted him

A Jap, with a rifle in his hand, appeared, followed by others.

135

with a smile. "Mind you, I'm admitting nothing. But—off the record—I'd advise you to reserve space in your obituary columns!"

"For Zambetta, Señor?"

Steve spread his hands. *"Quien sabe?* Just keep a blank space for the name of the victim!"

He shook hands with the reporters. "And now, if you'll excuse me, boys, I have an appointment to keep before I go to my room. I'll see you again perhaps."

Miguel Santos touched him on the shoulder. "Señor Klaw, a word in private, if you please." He drew Steve aside. "First, I must tell you that I am a loyal citizen of Chile. I believe that the future of our country here depends upon defeating the Axis, and there are thousands who think as I do. But we can accomplish nothing while the government refuses to declare war against the Axis. However, please count upon me, personally. I will do whatever I can to help you."

He paused, and his voice dropped to more confidential tones. "I have friends in North America, in Washington. I know that your work is more than only to find Zambetta. I know that it is an emergency which has brought you here, and that a great threat to your country exists from this Gaston Zambetta."

Steve raised his eyebrows. "You *are* pretty well informed, Santos."

The reporter smiled. "Your American shipbuilder, Barrett, has opened shipyards here in Valparaiso, as well as in Santiago. It is understood that he has a new process for building ships five times faster than usual. It is the threat to these shipyards which brings you here."

Stephen Klaw nodded soberly. "Your information is correct, Santos, as far as it goes. I'm admitting this to you, because I was told in Washington that you are one man we can trust. But I don't know exactly where or how the blow is going to fall. I'm working in the dark, till I hear more from Washington."

Santos was touched by Steve's confidence. "Whatever I learn, I shall tell you—depend upon that! I shall print not a word of this in my paper. Trust me, Señor Klaw!"

For a moment, the eyes of the two men met in mutual understanding. Then Steve said, "Thank you, Santos. I'll remember that."

He pressed the reporter's hand, and started for the doors which led to the street.

UP ON the balcony which ringed three sides of the lobby, there was a sudden flurry of motion. A face appeared at the railing, and alongside it the muzzle of a rifle.

A woman screamed somewhere, and the scream was immediately drowned out by the two gun shots which sounded almost as a single explosion. One came from the rifle up there on the balcony, and the other from the small automatic which Klaw had drawn from his right hand pocket.

The rifleman on the balcony hadn't had time to get set properly; he had been compelled to shoot without sighting too well. But Stephen Klaw had merely snapped his automatic up in a swift, free-arm shot.

The rifle bullet gouged the tiled floor almost at Klaw's feet, and ricochetted away. Steve's slug smashed squarely into the face of the assassin on the balcony. The rifle fell forward over the railing, and struck the tiled floor with a clatter.

Klaw made a wry face, and turned to the reporters, who thronged once more about him.

"A nice way to welcome a guy to your city!" he said to Miguel Santos.

"This is terrible, Señor Klaw!" Santos exclaimed. "It is a blot upon the name of the City of Valparaiso, upon the hospitality of the Republic of Chile. I shall denounce it to high heaven. It is these cursed Germans and Japanese!"

The local *policia* came swarming into the hotel in their natty uniforms. Some of them brought the body of the would-be assassin down from the balcony, while others surrounded Stephen Klaw.

A portly little man, in a uniform adorned with a good deal of gold braid, introduced himself as Colonel Garcia, Superintendent of the Police.

"You are to be congratulated upon your swiftness with the gun, Señor Klaw. I am mortified that this should have happened. Let me give you a police guard."

"No thanks, Colonel," Steve said dryly. "I'm pretty sure I can take care of myself."

Garcia blinked. He drew Steve to one side. "You do not understand, Señor Klaw!" He had begun to speak in English, but under the stress of his excitement he reverted to swift and fluent Spanish. "The assassin whom you just killed is a Japanese. He is known to the police, but we have refrained from taking action against him, because of his connection with the Japanese Consulate. Believe me, Señor Klaw, I know of your mission here. It is for the honor of your country that you seek him out, this Zambetta. But I warn you, Zambetta is the most dangerous man in South America today. He enjoys the assistance of the German and the Japanese embassies, which have much power here in Chile. They do not hesitate to kill when they fear an enemy—as you have cause to know. You will not be safe without police protection."

"Thank you, Colonel," Steve said politely. "I deeply appreciate your concern over me. But I would still prefer to do without it."

"No, no—please! This attempt will not be the last. Every moment that you remain in Valparaiso will be a moment of danger for you. Wherever you turn, there may be a knife waiting to be plunged into your back, or a hidden gun waiting to spit death at you. Even the food you eat may be poisoned. Every person who speaks to you may be an agent of Gaston Zambetta, eager to lure you to your doom. You *must* allow us to give you a guard!"

"No," said Stephen Klaw firmly.

Colonel Garcia shrugged with Latin expressiveness. "I have done my duty. I have warned you—I can do no more. I wish you luck!"

"Thank you again," said Stephen Klaw. "May I leave?"

"Go with God, Señor."

Steve nodded, and turned away. Still with his hands in his pockets, he headed toward the exit.

Colonel Garcia's eyes were clouded as he watched him go.

He turned and saw that Miguel Santos, of *El Nación,* was also watching Klaw's back. He sighed. "The man will he dead before morning."

"I wonder," Miguel Santos said thoughtfully. "I have heard many stories of this Suicide Squad, of which Klaw is one. I wonder if Gaston Zambetta—with all his power—should not be the one to worry at this moment!"

CHAPTER 2
DEATH IS A WOMAN

THE SUN was still warm and cheerful when Stephen Klaw emerged into the street. The *Avenida Bolivar* was teeming with a gay and careless throng, nationals of every country on the globe, spies and diplomats, merchants and refugees alike. But beneath that holiday atmosphere there was a curious sort of tension. Everyone was aware that Chile—as well as her neighbor, Argentina—could not forever hold out against the universal opinion of the millions of people in South America who hated the Axis, and who had already declared themselves against everything for which Hitler and Hirohito stood. It was as if this city were sitting upon a volcano which might be expected to erupt at any moment.

Klaw turned to the left on the Avenida Bolivar, still watchful and wary.

The first thing he noticed was an old-fashioned fiacre, hitched to the two superb Andalusian horses at the curb. The coachman was perched high up behind, attired in maroon livery.

But it was the occupant of the carriage who held Steve's attention. She was a young woman, perhaps twenty-six, dressed in black, and with a black lace mantilla about her head. Her face was thin; but the finely carved features were a mask of sheer beauty which left one breathless. Black eyes flashed at Stephen Klaw as she leaned close to the window. One long-fingered hand, encased in a black glove, was raised as she beckoned to him.

Klaw stopped a moment, then shrugged, and approached the fiacre.

Immediately, she opened the door. "Señor Klaw?"

He nodded.

"I must talk with you," she said hurriedly, with a faint Castilian accent. She looked around, as if fearful of being observed, then urged, "Come in quickly, please!"

Klaw grinned. He stepped into the carriage, and closed the door.

The woman moved over to make room for him. There was a deep, almost frightening urgency in her dark eyes.

"Señor Klaw," she said, "It is dangerous that I should be seen talking with you. But I must warn you. You are walking to your death!"

Klaw looked at her levelly. "It's nice of you to let me know."

She put a gloved hand out, gripped his arm. "They tell me you are an obstinate man, Stephen Klaw. And a very brave one. But I beg of you—give up this folly. Give up your search for Gaston Zambetta!"

Steve smiled, but he said nothing.

She studied his face for a moment, then she said, "Yes, indeed, they were right. You are a brave, obstinate man. You will not give up the search."

"No," said Steve. "I will not."

"Then I must help you."

"Why?" Steve asked.

A slight shadow passed across her perfectly chiselled, aristocratic face. "Never mind why. Is it not enough that I will help you?"

"How?"

"Come tonight. An hour before midnight. Come to Number 27, Calle San Obispo. Then I will tell you where you may find Gaston Zambetta and how you may destroy him!"

"Whom shall I ask for?" Steve inquired casually.

Her eyes flickered. She still held his arm. "The name is of no consequence. You may call me Dolores if you wish. But you must surely come to Number 27 San Obispo tonight."

"Do you think I'll live that long?" Klaw asked.

She stiffened. "What—what do you mean?"

STEVE TOOK her hand, and gently removed it from his sleeve. He held it by the wrist. She had closed her hand into a fist, but he said, "Open it," in a smooth, soft voice.

She stared at him for an instant, and her face went white. Slowly, she opened her hand. The palm of the black glove was thickly covered with a bright red paste of some kind.

"Very clever, my dear Dolores," said Steve.

She was watching him with bright, wide eyes, but she made no attempt to release her wrist.

142

Steve chuckled, let go of her hand, and twisted his arm around, so that he could see the back of his sleeve. Sure enough, there was a bright red smudge of the paste, about five or six inches above the elbow.

"It stands out like a beacon, doesn't it?" he said.

"I am sorry," she whispered. "It—it was—I must have accidentally crushed my lipstick—"

Klaw shook his head. "Cut it, kid. You did it deliberately. You marked me so that Gaston Zambetta's hired killers will have no trouble in identifying me in the crowded streets of Valparaiso!"

"No—no! You are mad!" she exclaimed.

"I'm not stupid!"

His hand went into his coat pocket. The girl's eyes widened, and she tensed. She snapped open her handbag, and snatched at a small pistol inside. But once more, Stephen Klaw reached out and gripped her wrist. He held her helpless that way, until she sighed, and let go of the pistol. It dropped back into the bag.

Her eyes were fixed on the pocket in which Klaw had his hand, as if she dreaded to see him bring out a gun.

"Are you going to—kill me?"

Steve shook his head. "I don't make war on women. But you can give Gaston Zambetta a message for me. Tell him to come after me himself—instead of sending women to do his dirty work!"

She closed her eyes for a moment. When she opened them once more, there was a strange softness in them.

"I will give Zambetta your message, Stephen Klaw. It is too bad that we cannot be friends. But I must be your enemy so long as this war lasts. I shall work hard to trap you, just as you will work hard to trap Zambetta. May the best man win!"

"Fair enough," said Stephen Klaw.

She smiled wryly. "Zambetta will be angry when he learns that I have failed to mark you. He has already issued orders that the man with a red mark upon his arm is to be killed on sight. I suppose you will wipe it off—"

"Why no," said Stephen Klaw. "I'll not wipe it off. You can tell Gaston Zambetta to let his order stand. Since Zambetta is too yellow to come to me himself, I must make it easy for his hired men to find me—so they can lead me to *him!*"

She gazed at him, her lips parted, a strange look in her face. "You *must* be mad!"

SHE CLOSED the door and leaned back, and snapped a sharp command in Spanish into the speaking tube. The coachman cracked his whip, and the horses started off, leaving Klaw at the curb.

He gazed after the carriage, with eyes narrowed speculatively.

A big red-headed American, with shoulders like a stevedore's, lurched into him and said, "Excuse me," in a loud and resonant voice.

"It's all right," Steve said, without even glancing at the man. Then he added swiftly in an undertone, "Follow that dame, Johnny!"

"Right, Shrimp!" said Johnny Kerrigan. He grinned, looking at the red smudge on Steve's sleeve. "That's a hell of a place for a dame to kiss you, Shrimp!"

"Nuts to you, Mope," said Steve. "That is a method of identi-fication—so Gaston Zambetta's boys can find me easily."

"Very nice," said Kerrigan. "I hope you see them first. You don't have to worry, though. Dan Murdoch is keeping you covered."

Kerrigan moved away, and climbed into a cab in front of the hotel. A moment later his cab was off, on the tail of the carriage.

Steve didn't look around to try to spot Murdoch. It was enough for him that Kerrigan had said that Murdoch was there. He had taken it for granted that both his partners would be on deck and ready for action when he arrived, because that had been the arrangement, made in Buenos Aires three days ago.

And these three men—Kerrigan and Murdoch and Klaw—had worked so long together that they functioned like a perfectly integrated army corps. Each knew that he could count on the others, unless death intervened. It was never necessary for one of them to "make sure" that the others were on the job.

No other three members of the F.B.I. enjoyed exactly the same position. They were known as the Suicide Squad, and with good reason. They never rated a routine assignment, but were held in reserve for those jobs which the Director of the F.B.I. decided were far too dangerous for ordinary agents. Originally, there had been five men on the Suicide Squad. Then one day, there had been four; then only three. Tomorrow there might be but two, or one, or none.

But that was the way it must be. They wanted a fast life and a hard one, with the odds always big against them, and the stakes even bigger. No routine investigations or tiresome searches after bank defaulters or undesirable aliens for them. They had chosen adventure, which carried with it each moment the chance of instant death.

They had been handed this assignment in Washington, exactly fourteen days ago. All they had to do was to find Gaston Zambetta, the fabulous Axis spy responsible for more sinkings of Allied ships than any other agency. Operating from the safety of a neutral country, the tentacles of his organization spread out over all of Latin America. He had left the United States after murdering a young F.B.I. agent, callously leaving him, wounded, to die in a burning shack. Ostensibly, the Suicide Squad was down here to square up for that killing. In reality, their job was to crack open the entire Zambetta organization.

It was like striking flint against flint, the Suicide Squad against the Zambetta combine. Both were hard; both were unyielding, made of material that might break but would never bend. Among those of the diplomatic corps who knew the inside facts, bets were being made on the outcome. The odds offered were heavy against the Suicide Squad, because they were only three against countless numbers.

But one thing was sure: if Kerrigan, Murdoch and Klaw went down to death in Valparaiso, they would not go alone. They would take a goodly number of enemies to hell with them....

CHAPTER 3
"FIRE!"

STEVE KLAW hailed a passing cab and ordered in Spanish, "The United States Consulate, please."

But the taxi driver only looked at him with frightened eyes. "But no, Señor. I cannot take you." His glance whipped to the red smudge on Klaw's sleeve, and he hastily crossed himself.

"What?" Steve demanded.

The man threw in the clutch of his machine. "The Señor bears the mark of Zambetta!" And without another word, the fellow drove off-Steve chuckled. He hailed two more cabs, with the same result. At last he got a third taxi, driven by a fierce-looking fellow with a pock-marked face. This one didn't seem to be worried about the mark of Zambetta.

Steve got in and said, "The United States Consulate."

Steve's cab turned left from the waterfront and began to climb a steep road cut in the hills. Steve didn't say anything, although he knew that the United States Consulate was down along the beach—and this cab was going away from the beach!

Five minutes later, the cab swung into a side road, high above the city. Valparaiso is built almost literally on a mountain side. The business section is down below at the beach, but the residences, and many of the institutional buildings—which include the Chilean Naval Academy—are on the hills which surround the city like ramparts, and are reached by cable elevators which rise steeply from the business section below. Of recent years

147

however, beautiful auto roads have been cut in the hills, so that the residential heights are easily reached by car.

It was one of these highways which Steve's driver took, now. He sped past the wealthy residential mansions, then swung off the highway into a narrow dirt road which brought them out practically to the edge of a cliff, high over the city.

The cab came to a stop in front of a small white house which looked as if it had been long vacant.

Steve kept both hands in his pockets. He said with assumed innocence, "This can't be the United States Consulate."

The driver turned around, grinning wickedly over the long-barrelled revolver he held. At the same time, he leaned on the horn with his elbow.

"No, Señor," he said in Spanish. "This is not your Consulate. For you, it is the last destination in life!"

IN RESPONSE to his horn, the door of the little white house was flung open, and three wiry little Japs emerged, each carrying a short carbine. They wore dun-colored uniforms, steel helmets, and armbands on which was the insignia of the rising sun.

The driver grinned, indicating them. "It is the firing squad for you, Señor. Zambetta's firing squad."

One of the Japs opened the door of the cab, and motioned jerkily for Klaw to get out.

Steve looked at the cab driver, then at the three riflemen. "My executioners?" he asked.

"Exactly, Señor. You will face the wall of that house, and be shot in the back. Then your body will be hurled down the hill into the streets of Valparaiso for everyone to see that whoever else challenges Zambetta will die!"

"H'm," said Steve. "I don't like it. I was never shot in the back before."

"This will be the last time, Señor!" The cab driver laughed.

The Jap at the door was impatient. He thrust his carbine in, to poke at Steve.

Steve said softly, "You shouldn't do that!" and he shot the Jap with the automatic in his right-hand coat pocket. He fired through the cloth, without taking the gun out, and a neat round hole appeared in the Jap's forehead.

The other two riflemen frantically swung their carbines around to bear on Klaw, but Steve kept on shooting, grimly, and both men went down, without firing a shot. Klaw swung around to the cab driver, but it was unnecessary to worry about him, for that person was being taken care of, quite efficiently. He was sitting very still, with his hands above his head, a revolver muzzle at his ear.

Dan Murdoch was holding the revolver.

"Hi, Shrimp," Murdoch said casually, after the echoing thunder of the gunshots had died away. "That was nice shooting. I enjoyed watching you."

"Hi, Mope," said Steve. "Where did you come from?"

Murdoch grinned. "I rode right up the hill with you—on the back bumper. Down in the city, people looked at me as if I was nuts, but then they think all Americans are whacky, anyway."

He wiggled his revolver against the cab driver's ear.

"Descend, *amigo,*" he ordered. "We're going to have a little conference."

The cab driver, still with his hands in the air, got out of the car. Steve climbed out, picking his way among the bodies of the Japs. The three men made their way to the house.

There was no one else inside. They found a radio receiving set, and a night semaphore outfit, for signalling to ships at sea.

Murdoch said, "This looks like one of Zambetta's communication spots."

"Let's fix it for him."

Steve took out a packet of matches, and went around, applying flame to everything that would burn. Soon the fire was roaring through the shack.

The cab driver watched him sourly, his face setting obstinately when Murdoch asked him questions. He began edging toward the door as the heat of the fire became uncomfortable.

But Dan Murdoch kept him inside, at the point of the revolver, while Stephen Klaw went out and busied himself with the bodies of the Japs. Steve came back in a few moments, with three belts, which he had taken from the dead men.

"Turn around!" Steve ordered.

The cab driver's face paled. "What are you going to do, Señor?"

"Don't worry," Murdoch told him. "We're not going to shoot you."

"Of course not," said Steve. "We're just going to strap you up, and leave you here in the shack."

"But—but it is *burning!*"

"How observant you are."

"You—you will leave me to be burned alive?"

"That's the general idea," Steve told him. "Now be nice and turn around."

"No, no!"

"Listen," Stephen Klaw said coldly. "You work for Gaston Zambetta. He fled from the United States a couple of months ago. He left an agent of the F.B.I. to be burned to death in a boathouse on the Florida coast."

"And what's sauce for the goose," Dan Murdoch explained, "is sauce for the gander!"

The cab driver's face became white, his eyes desperate. He lunged frantically toward the door, but Murdoch caught him in an arm-lock, and held him helpless, while Steve proceeded to fasten one of the belts on his wrists.

"For the love of mercy," the wretch begged, "do not do this to me!" He cringed as the flames licked closer and closer to the spot where they stood. "Spare me! I will do anything!"

STEPHEN KLAW stopped in the act of fastening the belt. His eyes met those of Murdoch, and there was relief in both of them. If the wretch had only known them better, he could have guessed that it was only a bluff on their part.

But Murdoch's voice was cold and hard as he spoke to the fellow. "I'm sorry, but you must burn, to even up the score for Jerry Henderson."

"Please—"

"Wait," said Steve suddenly, as if trying to persuade Murdoch. "Couldn't we give this guy a break?"

"Hell, no! Why should we?"

151

"Maybe he could help us get a line on Zambetta. He works for him. Perhaps he would betray his master for the sake of his miserable life."

The fire was now so hot it was almost unbearable. In a moment they would have to get out.

"I dare not betray Zambetta!" the wretch screamed. "He will kill me."

"See?" said Murdoch. "He won't play ball with us. Come on—hurry this up. Tie him, and let's get out."

"Wait, wait!" the frightened man screamed. "Do not leave me here. Wait! I—I will do—" his voice caught, and he whispered, "I will do whatever you ask!"

"All right," said Murdoch, as if relenting unwillingly.

They dragged the trembling cab driver out into the open air. The sweat was thick upon his face, and he was shivering as if he had the ague.

"Talk!" Murdoch ordered. "Talk fast, and say something worth while—or you go back in the fire!"

"Ask what you wish to know. I will tell everything."

"What's your name?"

"Diaz. Julio Diaz."

"How do we get to Zambetta?"

"That I do not know, Señor."

"Nuts!" Murdoch said disgustedly. "Put him back in!" He increased pressure on the arm-lock, and thrust the man toward the roaring inferno.

"Wait!" shrieked Diaz. "Wait! I—I can tell you!"

Murdoch stopped. "Well?"

The fellow was gasping with fright. His voice caught in his throat, but he managed to say, "I—can tell you how I report—to Zambetta. I swear, Señores, that I do not know where to find Zambetta. There are hundreds like me in Valparaiso, who obey orders, but who know nothing. We receive our orders through a third party."

"Go on," said Murdoch.

"At 27 Calle San Obispo," the fellow gasped. "There is a book store. I go there every day, and look in a certain book—*Don Quixote*—where I find my orders on a slip of paper. If I have a report, I write it and place it within the book. There are others like me, who also come to the book store for orders. Each has one certain book."

"27 San Obispo!" repeated Steve Klaw. "That's where the dame told me to go tonight!"

Murdoch shook the trembling Julio Diaz. "What else do you know, *amigo?*"

"That is all. I swear it!"

"Who pays you?"

"I find my pay in the book."

Murdoch looked over at Klaw. "What do you say, Shrimp? Think he's telling the truth?"

"It is the truth, Señores! I swear it is the truth!"

Steve shrugged. "We'll find out soon enough. Let's give him the benefit of the doubt. If he's been making up fairy stories for our benefit, we can always start another fire...."

Murdoch said, "Let's get going before the department arrives."

They bundled the trembling Diaz into the cab, and Murdoch took his cap and badge; got behind the wheel. Klaw sat next to their captive, while Murdoch headed the cab back down into town.

On the way, they passed two fire engines. The flames from the burning shack were lancing upward, high over the hills, plainly visible to those in the city below. Zambetta, wherever he was, would know that something had gone wrong with his projected execution of Stephen Klaw.

Murdoch chuckled. "Maybe the Jap submarines out at sea will think that's a signal for them!" Then he asked over his shoulder, "Where to, Señor?"

"The United States Consulate, James," Steve said with a grin. "And don't you take me for any rides!"

CHAPTER 4
IGPAY ATINLAY

THEY HERDED their prisoner up the back stairs of the Consulate building, into the consul's office. By this time it had become dark, and the chill wind from the sea was sweeping in over the city.

The Consul stared with ill-concealed dismay at Klaw and Murdoch and their prisoner.

"What do you chaps think you're doing? Don't you realize that you've violated about a dozen laws of the Republic of Chile? You're guilty of arson, kidnapping—"

154

"What did you want me to do?" Klaw demanded. "Let those Japs stand me against a wall and fill me full of lead?"

"I can't have anything to do with this," the Consul insisted. "Our relations with Chile are friendly. I can't lend myself to violating her laws!"

"But it's all right for Zambetta to violate her laws, eh?" Murdoch asked bitterly.

"All we want you to do," Stephen Klaw explained patiently, "is to keep this guy Diaz safely and secretly in some dark room, so he can't communicate with Zambetta. We want Zambetta to be in doubt about what happened up at that shack."

"Sorry," said the Consul. "I can't do it. I must turn this man loose. But as for you two, you may remain here. As you know, this Consulate building enjoys diplomatic immunity. You may hide here, and you will be safe from prosecution. Also, you will be safe from Zambetta's vengeance."

Dan Murdoch uttered a snort of disgust. "You can take your diplomatic immunity and shove it up your chimney!" he said hotly. "All the immunity *we need is this!*" He tapped the bulge where his revolver rested snugly in its holster.

He sprang up, and jerked his thumb at the cowering Julio Diaz. "Scram!" he said. "Get out of here, and hide that ugly mugg of yours in some Valparaiso sewer. Don't get under our feet again, or you'll get the works!"

Diaz hurried toward the door. "I am finished with Zambetta, Señores. No more will I work for him. I think Zambetta will lose his battle with the Suicide Squad. *Adios, Señores!*"

He ducked out of the door, and disappeared.

Stephen Klaw got up.

"We might as well be going, too," he murmured. He looked at the Consul, who was carefully adjusting his pince-nez. "It's guys like you, mister, who give the other nations the idea that America is soft! You coddle these foreign diplomats, and let them get away with murder, and then after a while they walk all over you. That's why Zambetta is so powerful down here in Chile. He's ruthless, and he's not afraid to go after what he wants. So they respect him, and they respect the Axis. But they know they can step on *your* toes, and nothing will happen."

He paused, leaning over the desk, waggling a finger in the Consul's face. "Kerrigan and Murdoch and I are going to show them that they *can't* step on the toes of Americans!"

The diplomat was plainly flustered. He took off his pince-nez, and polished it nervously. "I wish you men would listen to reason. You'll only make trouble for yourselves, and end up in the morgue. You don't understand the procedure of diplomacy—"

"If pussyfooting is diplomacy," Klaw said, "give me gas-house gang tactics!"

HE SWUNG around to Murdoch. "Come on, Dan. Let's get out of here!"

"I warn you, Klaw," the Consul said, "that whatever trouble you get into will be on your own head. I will not lift a finger to help you."

He was interrupted by the ringing of the telephone on his desk. He picked it up and listened for a moment, then raised his voice to recall Steve and Dan, who were on their way out.

"It's Washington calling. They want to know if you have contacted me. They want to talk to one of you."

Klaw went over and took the instrument from him.

It was the Chief of the F.B.I. "Thank God I've been able to get you!" the Chief said. "I tried the Hotel Republica, and they told me you hadn't even gone up to your room. How are you doing?"

"So far so good, sir," said Klaw. "We have only committed arson, murder and kidnapping. But give us a chance. We're just beginners."

The Chief chuckled. "I expect you've been getting a lecture from the diplomatic corps?"

"And how!"

"Can't be helped, Steve. They still have to go by the book."

"But not us, sir!"

"Just don't get yourselves killed unnecessarily. I'd hate to have the expense of shipping your bodies back here, all the way from Valparaiso. Now listen carefully. I have something to tell you—something important. But I'm sure the Consulate wire there is tapped. It wouldn't do any good for you to call me back on long distance from another phone, either. They listen in on all the international calls. But I've got to tell you this—"

"Did you ever hear of pig-latin, sir?" Steve interrupted.

"Good Lord, Steve, it's forty years since I used pig-latin. But here goes!"

He took a breath, and then his voice came over the phone slowly, while Steve Klaw wrote: *"Ogay otay ewelryjay toresay rounda-ay ornercay romfay ouryay otelhay."* The Chief broke off for a moment and said, "Have you got it so far, Steve?"

157

Klaw was grinning as he wrote. He winked at Murdoch, who was silently laughing at the dazed expression on the Consul's face as he saw the apparently meaningless words which Klaw had written.

"Go ahead, sir," said Klaw. "You're doing fine."

"Ontactcay irlgay amednay ianaday arretbay. Hesay ashay opeday bouta-ay ambettazay."

Steve finished writing and said, "Nice work, Chief! I've got it all down. We'll get right to work."

"Be careful, Steve," said the Chief. "This development may be bigger than your original job."

"You know us, Chief," Klaw said cheerfully. "We're always careful!"

The Director grunted. "Good luck!" and Stephen Klaw hung up, grinning.

The Consul was staring at the words Klaw had written on the paper.

"Code, isn't it?" he asked.

"Why no," Steve told him. "It's a language."

"A language? Impossible. What language?"

"Igpay atinlay!" Steve said. Then he took Murdoch's arm and they went out, leaving the Consul as perplexed as ever.

IN THE street, they hastily glanced at the note once more. Steve read it straight: *"Go to jewelry store around corner from your hotel. Contact girl named Diana Barrett. She has dope about Zambetta."*

"Diana Barrett!" said Murdoch. "Her father runs the Barrett Dry Dock in Baltimore and Newport News. He built shipyards in Chile and Argentina about five years ago, and he's been turning out ships down here, by a new process, for the United States. They say that by his new method, he can build a destroyer a month!"

"H'm," said Steve. "And Diana Barrett has opeday about ambettazay. Etslay ogay and see her."

"Don't look now," Murdoch said in a conversational voice, "but there a couple of apjays behind us!"

They had left the Consulate by the back way, and they were now in a dark side street. Only a few feet away there was the noise and the light of the busy avenue, but here the shadows were heavy.

"It's that damned Julio Diaz!" Steve said. "He must have gone straight to Zambetta when we let him go!"

His glance followed the slight motion which Murdoch made with his head, and he spotted the figures of two men, skulking in a doorway a few feet behind them.

"I think they're harmless for the moment," Murdoch said. "They're probably interested in where we're going. And what happened up in the Consulate."

"Shall we give them the old razzle-dazzle?" Klaw asked.

"Right," said Murdoch.

They kept on walking, not even turning to look back, until they emerged upon the avenue. Then, without signal or warning of any kind, Klaw and Murdoch parted. Klaw went to the left, Murdoch to the right. Each started walking rapidly.

Behind them, the two Japs came hurrying into the Avenue

and, seeing that their quarry had separated, they did likewise. One Jap took off after Murdoch, the other after Klaw.

The next few minutes would have been interesting, if seen from an airplane, with a clear view of two square blocks below. Klaw turned left at, the next corner, and Murdoch turned right at his corner, each with his shadow sticking like glue.

Then, coming around on the third side of their respective square blocks, Klaw made another left turn, and Murdoch another right turn, so that they were heading toward each other, and would meet at the side street from the other end of which they had started their respective circumnavigations of their respective blocks.

As they approached the corner, Steve could see Murdoch behind him, as Murdoch could see Klaw.

They met at the corner, but did not stop. They passed each other, walking swiftly, and before the two Japs could gather their wits, Klaw had come face to face with Murdoch's shadower, and Murdoch had come face to face with Klaw's man.

They both acted with the same degree of surprise and speed.

Steve Klaw winked at his Jap, said, "So sorry!" and feinted with his left. The Jap ducked, coming in low for a jiu-jitsu hold, and Steve's smashing right caught him a terrific blow in the temple. The fellow went down like a poled ox.

Murdoch's technique was slightly different, but no less efficient. He stepped up close to his Jap, and the fellow, seeing he was in for trouble, yanked a knife out from under his coat.

Murdoch said, "Naughty!" and jabbed an outstretched index finger straight at the Jap's eye. The knife-man twisted around to avoid that jab, and Murdoch caught his knife-arm by the back of the elbow. With his other hand he gripped the back of the Jap's neck, and propelled him forward with a mighty shove, at the same time sticking his own left foot out in front of the Jap's ankle. Under the impetus of the shove, the Japanese killer stumbled, tripped over Murdoch's foot, and fell heavily, face down, on the concrete. The knife slid out of his hand as his head struck with a nasty thud. He lay quite still.

Murdoch and Klaw turned away from their victims, faced each other, and grinned. They came back to the corner, linked arms, and walked complacently up the side street, without being tailed this time.

"I wonder," said Stephen Klaw, "if Johnny is having fun, too?"

"I wonder!" Dan Murdoch echoed smugly.

CHAPTER 5
ZAMBETTA'S MARK

THE JEWELRY store around the corner from the Republica Hotel was no more than a hole in the wall, in a block of stores. The lettering on the window said:

SALAZAR y COHEN

English Spoken

Klaw and Murdoch passed it by once, without going in. But they peered through the window, and could see no sign of a girl waiting there. All they could discern was a bald-headed man seated over a watch-repair bench.

Two or three men turned to look at Steve as they walked down the street, past the shop of Salazar y Cohen. It was the red smudge on Steve's sleeve that attracted the attention.

Murdoch grinned. "How's it feel, being a marked man, Shrimp? Why don't you wipe that thing off?"

"Nix," said Klaw. "I told the dame, Dolores, that I'd keep it on. You wouldn't have me break my word to a lady, would you?"

Murdoch suddenly snapped his fingers. "You wouldn't believe it, Shrimp, but I've got an idea!"

They were passing a cosmetic shop, a few doors down from the jewelry store, and Murdoch came to an abrupt halt, staring at the window display. Then he turned and looked at Klaw, and they both smiled.

"You've got something there, Mope!" said Steve.

The two of them went into the cosmetic store, and a few minutes later they emerged, while the dazed proprietor of the shop stared after them, shaking his head.

They did not at once return to the jewelry store of Salazar y Cohen, but they moved down into the busy *Avenida Bolivar,* and mingled with the crowds. The throngs were becoming thicker now, and Klaw and Murdoch seemed to be in a good deal of a hurry, walking as swiftly as possible, taking each man they over- took by the arm, and apologizing for jostling him out of the way.

It was significant that they seemed only to jostle Germans and Japs. Thus, they hurried along the *Avenida Bolivar* for several blocks, and then turned into the Trans-Andean Railway Station, where it was even more crowded.

They worked their way out the north exit of the station,

followed another street back to the *Avenida Bolivar,* and at last reached the jewelry store of Salazar y Cohen once more. They glanced down at the palms of their hands, which were bright red with the lipstick they had purchased in the cosmetic shop.

In their short excursion they had placed the red smudge on the sleeves of at least a hundred assorted Germans and Japs. As they stood there, they could see several men passing, with the mark.

"That ought to help a lot!" Murdoch said with a satisfied smirk. "Zambetta's killers will have a nice batch of marked men to kill. I bet there'll be quite a few dead Germans and Japs by morning!"

Steve chuckled. "You're a genius, Mope."

"I got the idea out of Ali Baba and the Forty Thieves," Dan admitted modestly.

They wiped the red stuff off their hands and went into the jewelry store of Salazar y Cohen.

THE LITTLE bald-headed man got up from his bench, and came over. *"Buenas noches, Señor,"* he said to Steve, who was in the lead. *"Com' esta Usted?"*

"I'm all right," Steve said in English. "How are you?"

The bald-headed man looked blank. *"No comprende."*

"You don't understand?" Steve repeated, in Spanish. "But your sign says English is spoken here."

"Of a surety, Señor. *Aqui se habla Inglès."*

"But you *don't* speak English."

"The sign does not say that I speak English, Señor. It is my partner, Cohen, who speaks the English."

"Where is he?"

"Dead, Señor."

"I give up," said Steve, in English.

Murdoch grinned. "You are the other partner—Salazar?"

"Indeed, yes, Señor. Gabrielle Salazar, at your service. You wish, perhaps, to purchase a watch? Or to have one repaired?"

"No," said Steve. "I wish to speak to a young lady named Diana Barrett."

Señor Gabrielle Salazar's face went blank once more. "As you can see, Señor, there is no young lady here."

"Is there any other jewelry store on this street?" Murdoch demanded, still in Spanish.

"No, Señor."

Steve and Dan looked at one another, perplexed. "The Chief couldn't have given us a wrong steer, could he?" Klaw said thoughtfully.

"Not he," said Murdoch. "And you got that pig-latin down right. I could hear his voice over the receiver. If the Chief said that girl was here, then she must be here."

Señor Salazar stood looking at them blandly, apparently unable to comprehend their language.

"I smell something rotten," Steve said suggestively.

"Me too," said Dan.

"Let's investigate the smell," Steve suggested.

"Okay," agreed Murdoch.

Steve put both hands in his pockets. "I think this guy is taking us for a ride," he said in English. "We ought to see what he has in the back of the store. It might be interesting."

"I'll take a look," said Dan.

But before he could move, the bald-headed Señor Salazar sprang behind the counter, and snatched up a wicked-looking Lüger.

"No you don't!" he growled in excellent English, except for a faint accent. "Stand right where you are!"

Steve said, "Tut, tut!" And once more today, he fired through his pocket. The muffled report sounded hardly louder than the cracking of a carriage whip. The slug caught the bald-headed man in the shoulder, and spun him around.

Working as if on a split-second timetable, Dan Murdoch stepped in even as Steve fired, and snatched the Lüger out of the bald-headed man's hand.

At the same time, Steve Klaw swivelled toward the curtained doorway at the rear. He fired three times, fast, still from his right-hand pocket, at the two yellow men who came pushing through, with guns in their fists.

HIS SHOTS smashed them backward through the curtained doorway, and he charged in after them, with his gun ready, in case there should be more.

Dan Murdoch swung around, stepped over to the door, and locked it. Then he pulled down the Venetian blind over the glass panel, and did the same for the plate-glass window.

From the rear, he heard Stephen Klaw calling to him. "Hey, Mope! Come here and see what we won!"

Murdoch paused only a moment to kneel beside the bald-headed man and make sure he was unconscious, then he hurried into the back room, stepping over the bodies of the two Japs in the doorway.

The inside room was small, and illuminated only by a weak bulb in a low floor lamp. But the lamp furnished enough light to show everything in the room.

One white man lay dead, sprawled on his face on the floor. In the opposite corner, a man and a girl were sitting on the floor, with their backs to the wall, both securely gagged and cruelly tied, hand and foot. The girl was young and fresh-complexioned, with a wealth of rich blond hair that fell freely over her shoulders.

Klaw and Murdoch cut the bonds that tied the two prisoners, and helped them remove the gags.

The girl was staring in horrified fascination at the body of the white man, which lay sprawled on the floor.

"That's Mr. Cohen," she told them. "The Japs came in here while I was waiting for you. They killed poor Mr. Cohen, and overpowered Mr. Salazar, here. Then they tied us both up, and planted that terrible bald-headed man out there to wait for you."

"You're Diana Barrett?" Steve asked.

She nodded, and covered her face with her hands. Sobs wracked her slender body.

"There, there," said Dan Murdoch, patting her shoulder. "This is no time to get soft."

Diana Barrett took her hands from her face, wiped her eyes. "I'm sorry," she said.

Salazar had seated himself, and was staring blankly at the

body of his dead partner. "Ten years we have been together in business," he muttered in Spanish. "And now he is dead!"

"Mr. Cohen was an American," Diana Barrett explained. "He came down here ten years ago, and went into partnership with Mr. Salazar. My father financed them. And now, when I was in trouble, I came here to hide in their back room. It was while I was here that I put in the long distance call to a friend of dad's in New York, and asked him to call Washington. He phoned me back and said that Washington would contact three F.B.I. men who were in Valparaiso, and would have them come here."

"I see," said Murdoch. "Zambetta must have had you followed. He knew you were here, and sent his Jap killers in to lay a trap for us!"

"What kind of trouble are you in?" Steve asked her.

She looked queerly at Murdoch and Klaw. "I don't see how you can help. There are only two of you, and this is something that would take the whole Marine Corps to accomplish."

"LISTEN, DIANA," Steve said, "don't waste time worrying about the Marine Corps. They are busy right now. We're taking over for them. Just give us the story—you'd best talk fast. Don't forget, if Zambetta knows we're here, there's nothing to stop him from sending a whole brigade of his Jap killers to try and wipe us out. So the sooner we get you out of here, the better."

"All right," she said, "this is the situation. You know who my dad is, of course?"

"He's the shipbuilder," said Murdoch.

"Yes. He has been operating four shipyards, two in Argentina, and two in Chile. One of them is here in Valparaiso. His new process permits him to build destroyers faster than mosquito boats could be built under the old system."

"We know all that," said Murdoch impatiently. "Get to the rest. Why did you call for help?"

"I have a younger sister," Diana hurried on. "Joan is thirteen years old. Yesterday—" Diana paused, and her voice choked up a bit—"yesterday, Joan was seized as she was coming home from the American School. A truckload of Japs pulled up alongside our car, overpowered the chauffeur, and took her away."

"Last night," Diana continued, "dad received a message from Zambetta. It was an ultimatum. Dad must sell out his four ship-yards to a Japanese shipbuilding firm before midnight tonight—or we'll never see Joan alive again!"

"The yellow devils!" Murdoch whispered softly.

"It's that terrible Zambetta!" Diana Barrett exclaimed. "He's part Japanese himself, and part Italian, and he has the soul of a fiend. Dad is waiting in the shipyard office until midnight. He doesn't dare go to the Valparaiso police, because he's afraid Zambetta will kill Joan immediately. Dad'll have to sign at midnight!"

"Sign away four big shipyards to the enemy?" Murdoch said. "Like hell he will!"

He took Diana by the arm, and helped her into the front of the store. Klaw followed, with Salazar.

The bald-headed man was still unconscious. Steve knelt beside him, and went through his pockets. But there were no papers on his person, or anything by which to identify him.

Steve got up, grimacing with disgust. "We'll leave him here. He's no good to us. Let's be going."

"Where?" asked Diana. "What can you do between now and midnight? The Japs are already in the shipyard, waiting to take over. They're so sure of themselves that they've already drawn up complete blueprints for operating the plant themselves. How can you two men stop them?"

"By getting your sister back," Dan Murdoch told her.

Her eyes shone eagerly. "You—you really think you can do it?"

"Maybe. Maybe not. But we can try!" "Two men against so many...." "That's where you're wrong, Diana," Steve told her. "There's more than two of us. There's three!"

CHAPTER 6
ONE MAN SHOW

CALLE SAN OBISPO was a rather busy thorough-fare down at the south end of the city, on the spur of land which stretched out along the south side of the harbor, far out to where the *Punta Angeles* lighthouse pointed upward like a warning finger at the sky.

Stephen Klaw moved warily down this, street, seeking Number 27, which was the address the woman, Dolores, had given him.

It was only eight o'clock, three hours earlier than the appointment she had made. But Klaw knew that the appointment was nothing but a trap, to be sprung in case every other effort to destroy the Suicide Squad failed. He was not here now to keep his date. He was seeking Johnny Kerrigan.

With the prospect of action in sights Kerrigan would never have forgiven Murdoch and Klaw if they had left him out of it. And Steve figured that if Kerrigan had stuck to Dolores' trail, he might have ended up at 27 San Obispo too.

There were a number of stores and cheap cinemas along this street. The shipyards and the docks were located down this way, and the streets were filled with shipyard workers and sailors of many nations. Over all the noises of the crowd there came the constant thrumming of machinery from the shipyards, and the clang of metal upon metal as the work of construction continued, twenty-four hours a day.

To the right, on the harbor side of the *Punta Angeles* peninsula, there was the vast, sprawling layout of the Barrett Shipbuilding corporation, with its great dry-docks, where destroyers were being rushed to completion on American orders. But after midnight tonight—provided Kerrigan and Murdoch and Klaw failed in their utmost hopeless effort—those great facilities might be working for the Japanese.

As Steve approached Number 27, he saw a crowd gathered in the gutter, and quite a number of the *policia* bustling officiously about. He paused at the edge of the crowd, peered over a woman's shoulder.

The object of the crowd's curiosity was a man who lay dead on his face, the upper part of his head shot off.

Everybody was talking excitedly in rapid Spanish, and Steve caught the name of Zambetta, several times.

The woman in front of him was saying to a companion, "I saw the poor man killed! In the very act of crossing the street, he was shot down from the doorway there!"

Steve's glance went to the dead man's sleeve. There was a red smudge upon it. He was one of those whom Murdoch and Klaw had marked.

The woman in front of Steve was saying, "See, the poor man has the mark upon him. All in the city know that this is the work of Zambetta. It has been said that there are three brave ones who have come from *America del Norte*, and that Zambetta has ordered his men to kill without mercy the ones who are thus marked!"

Steve's lips twisted in a faint smile.

The woman went on. "This must be one of those three brave men. They should have known that it was hopeless to fight Zambetta. I weep for them. It is a disgrace that those German and Japanese pigs should be so free to kill, here in Valparaiso. For my part, I would wish that we should enter the war by the side of the others!"

Steve touched her on the shoulder. She turned to stare at him.

"Thank you, madam," he said in excellent Spanish. "I am glad to hear such words from the lips of a Chilean woman!"

The woman's eyes were suspicious. There were many government spies in the streets these days, in the pay of the reactionary element, whom one dared not trust.

"Who are you?" she demanded, almost breathlessly.

Steve showed her the mark on his own sleeve. "I am one of those who fight Zambetta." Almost automatically, he lapsed into the flowery diction which the Latins love so much. "That dead man is not one of us. We have turned a little trick upon Zambetta. Tell your friends that the American Suicide Squad is still alive and fighting. And that Gaston Zambetta had better make arrangements for lodging in hell!"

THE WOMAN'S eyes glowed warmly. "God go with you, Señor. And may the Holy Virgin watch over you!"

Steve was touched by the woman's evident sincerity and emotion. He pressed her arm, and turned away without saying more.

On the fringe of the crowd, he found Johnny Kerrigan, who had spotted him talking to the woman.

"Hi, Shrimp," said Johnny. "I was waiting for you to come out of the huddle with the lady. What goes on here? I was watching that bookstore, from the rear, when I heard the shot. I came around and saw the guy with the red smudge on his sleeve, lying there. I thought at first it was you."

"No," said Klaw. "It's a German. Dan and I went around putting the smudge on a lot of Germans and Japs, and I guess Zambetta's killers have been having a field day all over town. Maybe by this time, Zambetta has given orders to lay off guys with red smudges on their sleeves, for fear of killing off the German and Jap population of Valparaiso!"

"Very nice going, Shrimp!" said Johnny. He took him by the arm and led him around the block, through an alley, and into a back yard behind the book store at Number 27 Calle San Obispo.

"This is where that dame in the carriage led me. I've been

keeping a watch ever since. From here, you can look right in through the store to the front. The dame went in there all right. She never came out, but I can't see her in there now."

Swiftly, Steve told him about Diana Barrett, and the Barrett Shipyard, and Diana's little sister, Joan.

"That dame holds the answers!" Kerrigan said. "We've got to find her!"

"We won't find her out here."

Johnny nodded. They moved over toward the rear entrance of the store.

"Where's Dan?" Johnny asked.

"He went to the Barrett Shipyard with Diana Barrett. If you and I fail to find Joan Barrett by midnight, Dan is supposed to stop the sale of the shipyard by hook or crook—even if he has to kidnap old man Barrett."

At the back door of the bookstore, Johnny tried the knob. The door opened under his touch, and they both stepped inside.

It was a long, narrow store, with shelves—loaded to the ceiling with books—on both long walls. There was a staircase in the rear, leading down to a basement, but they could see nothing down there, for it was pitch dark below.

The only person in the store was the proprietor, a stoop-shouldered old man in an alpaca jacket, with white hair parted in the middle, and a pair of thick-lensed glasses through which he peered nearsightedly at Klaw and Kerrigan.

WHEN HE saw the smudge on Steve's sleeve he smiled politely, and bowed low from the waist. He straightened, and the welcoming smile was gone from his face. There was a gun in his hand! It exploded without warnings as he pulled the trigger, but his aim at Klaw's heart was deflected by the heavy book which Johnny Kerrigan had yanked off the shelf and hurled at him. The book struck his gun wrist, and the shot buried itself in Gibbons' Decline and Fall of the Roman Empire, instead of in Stephen Klaw's body.

Before the man could shoot again, Kerrigan stepped in and struck down his arm, then clipped him one on the chin.

The man went down without a sound.

"Very well done, Johnny." said Steve. "I always said that the Dodgers lost good material when you joined the F.B.I. What did you throw at him?"

"I think it was Grimm's Fairy Tales," Johnny told him. "I didn't stop to look at the title."

He stooped and lifted the unconscious man, flung him over his shoulder like an inert sack.

"Lead the way, Señor Klaw!" he said, grinning.

Steve descended the stairs to the basement, with Johnny and his burden following. Steve moved down carefully and soundlessly, with a gun in one hand, and a flashlight in the other. His beam showed him that the basement was also lined with bookcases, containing old and musty tomes, thick with dust. But there was no living being down here.

"H'm," said Steve. "You said that dame, Dolores, came in here, and didn't leave. She's not upstairs, and she's not down here. And there's no door in here through which she could have gone."

"Therefore," Johnny Kerrigan said, standing and holding his burden with ease, "she must have gone through the *wall*."

"A very sensible deduction," Steve told him. He went around the walls, trying the various bookcases, feeling for hidden springs or secret buttons. Suddenly, he uttered an exclamation as he touched something and one of the bookcases began to move, soundlessly.

It opened out toward him, like a door, revealing a dark passageway beyond.

"So!" said Kerrigan. He put down the unconscious man, took off the fellow's belt and strapped his wrists with it. Then the two men moved to the darkness of that uninviting passageway.

The ceiling was low, the floor of crude and rotted planking. The air was dank with the tang of salt spray.

They followed Steve's questing flash-light beam.

"Boy," said Johnny, "this passage must be a hundred years old. I'll bet it's a relic of the old city, before the last earthquake!"

Steve said, "It leads down to the harbor!"

THE PASSAGE turned sharply to the right, and widened a bit. They continued on for another fifty feet, then Steve stopped short. He glanced down at the floor, saw the trapdoor there.

"Do we go ahead, or do we go down?" Steve asked.

"Wait a second," said Johnny. He took a coin out of his pocket. "Heads it's down, tails it's forward."

The coin came up heads.

Steve, moved aside, and Johnny bent over the trapdoor. There was an iron ring in it, nice and clean, and it moved easily, as if it were used frequently. Johnny got a grip on the ring and pulled, and the trapdoor came up.

There was nothing but darkness down below. Kerrigan took

out his flashlight and swung its beam through the opening. It disclosed an iron ladder which led down to a bare floor. It was a secret room of some kind, underneath the passageway.

"Me, first," said Johnny.

"Nix," said Steve. "Me first."

"Listen, Shrimp," Johnny growled. "You've been getting all the gravy since we hit Valparaiso. It's my turn now."

"I'll toss you for it," Steve suggested.

"Not on your life!" Johnny said. "You've won every time we tossed. That coin of yours must have two tails."

He pushed Steve aside, and climbed down the iron ladder. Steve followed, his automatic held ready. They sent their lights beaming all around the bare room.

There was no furniture in the room except for one chair, and an old army cot. On the cot lay a little girl, about twelve or thirteen, tied and gagged; staring at them fearfully out of big blue eyes.

"What do you know about that!" Johnny said softly.

Steve hurried over and untied the girl. He took the gag off.

"Don't be afraid, kid," he said. "We're friends. You're Joan Barrett, aren't you?"

She nodded. "The Japs brought me here. They've kept me tied up for I don't know how long!"

"It's all right now," Steve told her. "We'll get you back to your dad and your sister."

"Be careful," little Joan said. "The Japs are in the next room. There's a lot of them—and they—they have a machine-gun!"

Just then, the door to which she was pointing was flung open.

A Jap, in full uniform of a field soldier, with a rifle under his arm, appeared, followed by another.

Johnny Kerrigan, who was nearest the door, snapped two swift shots at the Japs, and the impact of the bullets smashed them backward. The shots reverberated through the small room like concentrated thunder, and immediately there appeared half a dozen more Japs, clambering through the doorway.

Johnny Kerrigan and Steve Klaw sent shot after shot into the doorway, and cleared it momentarily, and Johnny sprang over and slammed it shut. He sought vainly for a lock, but there was none on this side. He leaned heavily against the door, reloading the gun as he did so, and turned to look at Klaw.

"This is it, Steve," he said. "If I let go the door, the Japs will sweep over us. It would be a nice fight, but we've got to get the girl out of here."

"One of us will have to stay," Steve said slowly.

Kerrigan nodded silently.

"I'll toss you—" he began.

Johnny smiled grimly, and shook his head. "No toss, Shrimp. This is my show. Get going, Shrimp."

Stephen Klaw didn't argue with his partner. They might kid around when there was nothing better to do. But when the right time came, they took what the fates offered, and didn't complain.

"So long, Johnny," Steve said, his face a mask of tight restraint.

"So long, Steve," said Johnny. "See you in hell."

"See you in hell, Johnny!"

Steve took little Joan's hand. "Come on," he said gruffly. He helped her up the ladder. Already, the Japs were pressing against the door.

CHAPTER 7
THE DEAD STILL FIGHT!

STEVE KNEW that Kerrigan couldn't hold them for more than a moment or two, and that when the door was forced open, Johnny would be overwhelmed by the flood of Japanese. But he didn't stop or look back. He had said his good-by, and he didn't trust himself to say another word.

This was the way the Suicide Squad had always expected it to happen. They would have preferred to go down, all three of them together, fighting shoulder to shoulder in a good fight, and taking as many of their enemies along with them as possible. But they had always known that there might come a time when one of them would have to give up his life for the others, and they had all made the solemn agreement, that when the moment arrived there would be no waste of talk, or of sympathy.

In life, they had wanted nothing more than the chance to fight a good fight, and in death they wanted no pity.

Steve reached the passageway behind little Joan, and urged her back through the dank corridor, toward the bookstore. All the time, he listened for the sounds that would tell him the end had come for his partner.

But they were around the bend in the passageway, and had almost reached the door of the bookstore cellar before the sound of the first shot reached them. Then there was a quick volley, followed by utter silence.

Steve closed his eyes, and stood still for a moment. When he opened his eyes, he saw that Joan was looking up at him.

She put her small hand in his big one. "Did—did they—kill your friend?"

Steve didn't answer. He led her into the bookstore cellar, then up into the street.

The crowd was still out there, around the body of the dead man. Steve guided Joan Barrett down to the far corner, without being observed. They found a cab, and he ordered its driver to take them to the United States Consulate. There was a light in the Consul's window, and Steve brought Joan straight up there.

For two minutes, he gave the Consul a verbal lashing which made that gentleman's ears burn.

"So I'm leaving Joan Barrett here," he finished. "She's the daughter of an American citizen. She's entitled to your protection. Do you understand? See that no harm comes to her. It means more than just the life of one sweet little girl. It means the safety of your country!"

He walked out then, not trusting himself to say more. He looked neither to the right nor the left when he emerged. If any of Zambetta's killers had been watching for him then, he might have been an easy target.

"And then again, he might not. For no matter how intense his own personal emotion might be, he was still a fighting man of the first quality.

He flagged a passing cab and said, "The Barrett Shipyard!"

Ten minutes later, he descended at the great gate behind which the drydocks were located. An armed guard patrolled at the gate, just inside, and Steve nodded in satisfaction when he saw that it was a white man. The Japs hadn't got possession of the place—Old Barrett hadn't signed yet. But when he did, the Japs would move in legally, and no power on earth could stop them from making Japanese battleships in an American shipyard.

Steve's eyes were cold and gray. Johnny Kerrigan had given up his life to save this shipyard for America, and he didn't intend that Johnny should have given up his life in vain.

"I've got to see Barrett," he told the guard. "Fast!"

The man nodded, and called a superior. It was the captain in charge of the guards. "You'll have to state your business, before you can be admitted," the captain of the guards informed him.

"Tell Barrett that Stephen Klaw is here to see him—about his daughter, Joan."

THE CAPTAIN of the guards went into a little shack adjoining the gate. He came out in a couple of minutes, shaking his head. "I'm sorry, Klaw, but Barrett isn't interested. He doesn't want to see you."

"You're crazy!" Klaw exclaimed. Suddenly, his eyes narrowed. "Did you speak to Barrett personally?"

"No. I talked to his secretary, Dolores Martinelli."

"Dolores!" Steve repeated. "Is she a dark-haired dame, with black eyes and a shape that could get her in the Follies?"

"You said it!" the captain agreed.

Steve groaned. "Listen, pal, what's your name?"

"O'Brien."

"All right, O'Brien. You're an American. At midnight tonight, old man Barrett is going to sign this shipyard over to the Japanese—if I don't see him. He thinks his daughter, Joan, is in their hands. That dame, Dolores Martinelli, is deliberately keeping him from receiving any messages until he signs. She works for Zambetta!"

O'Brien's eyes narrowed. "How do I know you're telling me the truth?"

Steve took out his wallet, and flashed his F.B.I. identification card. Though he had technically resigned, he still had his card.

O'Brien looked at the picture, then at the name. "Damn! When you said your name was Klaw, I didn't get it at first. You're one of the Suicide Squad!"

"That's right."

O'Brien opened the gate.

"Thanks," said Steve.

"I wondered why there are so many Japs around today," O'Brien said. "They're all over the place. Miss Barrett came in with a tall guy a little while ago, and went to the administration building. Then we heard some noise in there, but when I went to investigate, Dolores Martinelli told me not to bother."

Steve said, "The tall guy with Miss Barrett was Dan Murdoch. And I can imagine what the excitement was about!

"Where's your other partner—Kerrigan?"

"The last I saw of him, he was on the road to hell. Here's where I send a few of those yellow devils after him!" He caught O'Brien's arm. "How many men have you got here—guards, I mean."

"Twelve," said O'Brien. "But in a fight, we wouldn't have a chance. There must be fifty Japs in uniform around the place." He waved a hand toward the dimly-lighted dry-dock. "There's a ship ready to be launched, and we're waiting for word from Barrett, but no orders have come out of the administration building tonight. It's damned funny."

"Get your men together," Steve told him. "This, may be a finish fight. Are you game?"

"We're game, all right!" O'Brien said. "The boys are about fed up with taking lip from the damned Germans and Japs around here!"

"All right. Got any grenades?"

"A sackful in the shack."

"Get 'em out. Distribute them to the boys. And wait for the fireworks to start."

He left O'Brien, and hurried through the night toward the administration building. At the door there was another guard, but O'Brien had already telephoned ahead, and the guard passed Steve through.

"Be careful, Klaw," said the guard. "There's a bunch of the Japs out in back, behind the administration building, and a whole mess of them inside. It looks damned funny that Barrett should suddenly have taken up with the little yellow monkeys!"

Steve nodded, and went inside.

There was a long, cool corridor within, with office doors on either side, and a receptionist's desk. But no one sat at the receptionist's desk tonight. Instead, half a dozen Japs, in full army uniform, were standing in the corridor. It was perfectly legal for these Japs to wear their army uniforms here in a neutral country, for they were classified as "military attaches." Ostensibly, they served their embassy and consulates, but in reality, they were the nucleus of the army of occupation which Japan hoped soon to throw into the country of Chile.

When they saw Steve, they immediately moved forward, drawing their guns.

STEVE STOOD spraddle-legged, a thin smile on his face. He began to shoot through his pockets. His shots reverberated through the corridor as he cut the Japs down, one after the other, coldly, mercilessly, calculatingly. He didn't give them a chance to finish drawing their guns. He shot them down like dogs, thinking all the time of Johnny Kerrigan, and of Dan Murdoch.

The Japs fell like nine-pins, and Steve moved forward, still shooting, until not one of the uniformed figures remained standing. His lips were tight and hard. He stepped among the bodies, slipping fresh clips into his automatics, and just then a door opened, and the startled, cameo-like face of Dolores Martinelli appeared in the doorway.

Steve hurled himself against the door, thrusting it inward, and sent her spinning into the room. He kicked the door shut, and faced the occupants of the room, an automatic in each hand, a grim smile on his lips.

Diana Barrett was there, standing next to the desk at which sat her father, the president of the great Barrett Shipbuilding Corporation. In front of the desk stood a tall, saturnine man, with close-cropped black hair, and a pair of snake-like eyes. He had turned, half-startled, and there was a revolver in his hand.

183

Dolores Martinelli, under the impetus of the thrust which Steve had given her, spun into the room on her knees, and had bumped into that sallow-faced man.

That was the reason why the sallow-faced man's shot missed Steve. It missed him by an inch, and the sallow-faced man didn't get a chance to shoot again, because Steve fired a single shot, and it took the man in the stomach.

Steve had fired at the stomach deliberately, with intention to cause the most painful wound possible. For this sallow-faced man was Gaston Zambetta—-abductor of little Joan Barrett, who had put the mark of death on the Suicide Squad, and who had left a young federal agent in Florida to burn to death.

Klaw stepped to the writhing body of Gaston Zambetta. "When you get to hell, Zambetta," he said, "give my regards to Kerrigan and Murdoch. Tell them I squared up for them."

Then he looked up at Diana and her father. "Joan is safe," he said wearily. "She's at the Consul's office. You don't have to sign the shipyard over."

But Diana was at the window, motioning urgently for Klaw to join her. Steve stepped over the body of the writhing, groaning Zambetta, and went to the window.

"Look! Down there!" Diana exclaimed.

Steve followed her pointing finger, and his heart leaped. Kerrigan and Murdoch were down there, tied back to back. And a small Jap in uniform was standing, half a dozen feet away, with a rifle in his hand, as if awaiting a signal.

"They didn't kill Kerrigan in that underground room," Diana breathed. "They rushed him, and took him captive. When

Murdoch and I came here, the Japs seized me, and threatened to shoot me if Murdoch didn't surrender. That's how they got the two of them prisoner. They were going to shoot them when Zambetta gave the signal. He was only waiting for dad to sign over the shipyard, so he could taunt them with it before they died!"

Steve Klaw swung a leg over the window sill. It was only a short drop to the ground, and he landed on his feet like a cat. The Jap soldier with the rifle turned and saw him, swung the rifle around—

Steve's slug caught the fellow in the head, then Steve was racing over to where his two partners were standing. With his pocket knife he slashed the cords that tied them.

"Hi, Mopes," he said, matter-of-factly. Nothing of what he had felt during the last hour showed in his face, or sounded in his voice. But he didn't need to say anything.

"Hi, Shrimp," said Johnny Kerrigan.

"Hi, Shrimp," said Dan Murdoch.

That was all. Then they went to work. Steve handed Murdoch one of his automatics. Kerrigan bent down and picked up the dead Jap's rifle. Together, the three of them moved around toward the front of the administration building, where O'Brien and his dozen men were waiting, with the grenades.

Down by the drydock, where the ship was ready to be launched, the Japs were swarming. If they had heard the few odd shots from the administration building, they must have assumed that their own men had everything well in hand.

Certainly, they didn't know if it was lightning that struck

them, or a swift Pacific monsoon. Most of them were dead before they realized they were in a fight. The remainder were overwhelmed by the spectre of those three grim-faced killers who descended upon them in the vanguard of a dozen angry Americans. They threw down their weapons....

A HALF hour later, the great shipyard was back to normal, and Kerrigan, Murdoch and Klaw were in the office, kneeling over the dying Zambetta. His snake-like eyes burned with unholy hatred as he gazed up at the three men.

"You devils!" he whispered. Then a spasm of agony crossed his face, and he died.

Kerrigan, Murdoch and Klaw stood up solemnly, and looked at Dolores Martinelli, whom Diana had kept covered.

"Get out!" Klaw said. "I told you once that we don't make war on women. Get out and go back to whatever country spawned you. Just keep out of the western hemisphere!"

Dolores Martinelli turned and walked out of that office. But she didn't get very far. The Chilean police were waiting, just outside the door, to arrest her.

Colonel Garcia came in a moment later. "Señores," he said, "you are great caballeros. Some day our country will officially recognize that it owes much to you for what you have done today. In the meantime, as a private citizen, I offer you all that I own. Whatever you wish, it shall be yours!"

"I'll take you up on that, Garcia," Kerrigan said. "I want an ice-cold glass of good Milwaukee beer!"

"Us, too!" said Murdoch and Klaw together.

POPULAR HERO PULPS AVAILABLE NOW:

ACE G-MAN
- ❏ #1: The Suicide Squad Reports for Death — $14.95
- ❏ #2: Coffins for the Suicide Squad — $14.95
- ❏ #3: Shells for the Suicide Squad — $14.95
- ❏ #4: The Suicide Squad in Corpse-Town — $14.95
- ❏ #5: Wanted—In Three Pine Coffins — $14.95
- ❏ **NEW:** #6: The Suicide Squad's Dawn Patrol — $14.95

OPERATOR 5
- ❏ #1: The Masked Invasion — $13.95
- ❏ #2: The Invisible Empire — $13.95
- ❏ #3: The Yellow Scourge — $13.95
- ❏ #4: The Melting Death — $13.95
- ❏ #5: Cavern of the Damned — $13.95
- ❏ #6: Master of Broken Men — $13.95
- ❏ #7: Invasion of the Dark Legions — $13.95
- ❏ #8: The Green Death Mists — $13.95
- ❏ #9: Legions of Starvation — $13.95
- ❏ #10: The Red Invader — $13.95
- ❏ #11: The League of War-Monsters — $13.95
- ❏ #12: The Army of the Dead — $13.95
- ❏ #13: March of the Flame Marauders — $13.95
- ❏ #14: Blood Reign of the Dictator — $13.95
- ❏ #15: Invasion of the Yellow Warlords — $13.95
- ❏ #16: Legions of the Death Master — $13.95
- ❏ #17: Hosts of the Flaming Death — $13.95
- ❏ #18: Invasion of the Crimson Death Cult — $13.95
- ❏ #19: Attack of the Blizzard Men — $13.95
- ❏ #20: Scourge of the Invisible Death — $13.95
- ❏ #21: Raiders of the Red Death — $13.95
- ❏ #22: War-Dogs of the Green Destroyer — $13.95
- ❏ #23: Rockets From Hell — $13.95
- ❏ #24: War-Masters from the Orient — $13.95
- ❏ #25: Crime's Reign of Terror — $13.95
- ❏ #26: Death's Ragged Army — $13.95
- ❏ #27: Patriots' Death Battalion — $13.95
- ❏ #28: The Bloody Forty-five Days — $13.95
- ❏ #29: America's Plague Battalions — $13.95
- ❏ #30: Liberty's Suicide Legions — $13.95
- ❏ #31: Siege of the Thousand Patriots — $13.95
- ❏ #32: Patriots' Death March — $14.95
- ❏ #33: Revolt of the Lost Legions — $14.95
- ❏ #34: Drums of Destruction — $14.95
- ❏ #35: The Army Without a Country — $14.95
- ❏ #36: The Bloody Frontiers — $14.95
- ❏ #37: The Coming of the Mongol Hordes — $14.95

CAPTAIN COMBAT
- ❏ #1: The Sky Beast of Berlin — $13.95
- ❏ #2: Red Wings For the Blood Battalion — $13.95
- ❏ #3: Low Ceiling For Nazi Hell Hawks — $13.95

DUSTY AYRES AND HIS BATTLE BIRDS
- ❏ #1: Black Lightning! — $13.95
- ❏ #2: Crimson Doom — $13.95
- ❏ #3: The Purple Tornado — $13.95
- ❏ #4: The Screaming Eye — $13.95
- ❏ #5: The Green Thunderbolt — $13.95
- ❏ #6: The Red Destroyer — $13.95
- ❏ #7: The White Death — $13.95
- ❏ #8: The Black Avenger — $13.95
- ❏ #9: The Silver Typhoon — $13.95
- ❏ #10: The Troposphere F-S — $13.95
- ❏ #11: The Blue Cyclone — $13.95
- ❏ #12: The Tesla Raiders — $13.95

MAVERICKS
- ❏ #1: Five Against the Law — $12.95
- ❏ #2: Mesquite Manhunters — $12.95
- ❏ #3: Bait for the Lobo Pack — $12.95
- ❏ #4: Doc Grimson's Outlaw Posse — $12.95
- ❏ #5: Charlie Parr's Gunsmoke Cure — $12.95

THE MYSTERIOUS WU FANG
- ❏ #1: The Case of the Six Coffins — $12.95
- ❏ #2: The Case of the Scarlet Feather — $12.95
- ❏ #3: The Case of the Yellow Mask — $12.95
- ❏ #4: The Case of the Suicide Tomb — $12.95
- ❏ #5: The Case of the Green Death — $12.95
- ❏ #6: The Case of the Black Lotus — $12.95
- ❏ #7: The Case of the Hidden Scourge — $12.95

THE SECRET 6
- ❏ #1: The Red Shadow — $13.95
- ❏ #2: House of Walking Corpses — $13.95
- ❏ #3: The Monster Murders — $13.95
- ❏ #4: The Golden Alligator — $13.95

CAPTAIN ZERO
- ❏ #1: City of Deadly Sleep — $13.95
- ❏ #2: The Mark of Zero! — $13.95
- ❏ #3: The Golden Murder Syndicate — $13.95